THE ISLAND

Teri Hall

THE ISLAND

BOOK THREE
OF
THE LINE TRILOGY

THE LINE
AWAY
THE ISLAND

Thanks

This year has been, even in a series of rather difficult years, notable in its challenges. I've had to ask friends and family for help, which I gratefully received. This book would not exist without that help. I thank and appreciate you all.

But I want to thank one person in particular for the help I received this year. I want to thank **the person behind the white envelopes**.

I don't know if you are a friend or a stranger. I have to admit I don't really want to know, because I'm so far from out of the woods I cannot see a time where I can repay you. What I want to thank you for, besides the obvious, is that I never had to ask. You, in your kindness, just gave.

And that has worked two kinds of magic (or maybe I should say it has generated two kinds of hope, for doesn't all magic begin with hope?). The first is a very practical magic, to be sure. At the very moments when despair enveloped me, a white envelope would appear. It was an unasked for, unexpected *magic*, which made food materialize and made heating bills disappear.

The second kind of magic these white envelopes have worked is not such a practical one. I can't explain it very well. All I can really say is that this second kind of magic has made me see different things in strangers' faces—even in friends' faces. It has made me see the need there, when I might have missed it before. It's made me see the kindness. It's made me hope to be like you are, whoever you are. To help if I can, without being asked. To notice, and to care, and however I am able, to *do something about it.*

Ashore

Nipper crouched behind a clump of unfamiliar grass, motionless but ready, every muscle taut. His undercoat was still damp from the sea and he was cold. More urgent than the cold was hunger; after fighting the waves for so long, he needed food.

He didn't think about sliding along the bottom of the boat, frantically clawing for traction, or about losing his grip and being swept into the frigid water. He didn't relive the moment, swimming, when he'd felt the last of his strength draining from his legs, or the moment just after that, when he felt sand firm beneath his feet. That was all over. Now was the moment he thought of—now, and the warm blood-scent of the strange creature he stalked on this unfamiliar beach.

He had not seen a creature like it beforc, but it looked like he could eat it, once he got past the gray-furred skin. It was soft and fat, and had no sharp ends, at least as far as he could detect. That usually meant the thing was food. It waddled across some flat stones set into the sand, stopping every few seconds to raise its crinkled nose to the sky and sniff, its eyes squeezed shut as though it didn't use them for much anyway.

The stones were the thing that held Nipper back. He knew they weren't natural; they were too consistent for that. They formed a path, a trail leading through the sand to somewhere. Nipper didn't want to go on the path. The scent of strangers— a smell not unlike that of his Nandy, but not, not hers—hung heavy around it. His stomach spoke louder than his fear, though. He crouched even lower and waited for the moment when the creature stopped to sniff again. Then, gathering all the power he had left, he leapt.

Chapter 1

Rachel couldn't stop smiling. She watched Pathik's chest rise and fall, slow and steady, and she smiled. The sun, so welcome after the black gale of the night before, was shining on his face, gilding his eyelashes and casting great long spikes of shadow along his gaunt cheeks. He was right there, next to her. And he *breathed*. And she smiled.

He was alive. They were *all* still alive.

They were all still asleep, too, except for her. She looked around the hastily made campsite, marveling at the fact that they'd made it to dry land. That they were here, on Salishan, the fabled haven to which Indigo, Pathik's grandfather, had urged all of the Others to flee. She wished he could be here with them. She wished, more than anything, that she hadn't been the cause of his death.

Pathik's father, Malgam, lay next to Nandy, the woman who had helped him raise Pathik. Nandy's head was nestled on Malgam's shoulder and one of his arms wrapped around her waist, holding her close even in slumber. Rachel's own father, a man she had thought was lost to her forever, held her mother, Vivian, cradled in his arms in a similar fashion. Seeing the two of them together still made Rachel feel as though she was dreaming; her whole life had been spent thinking Daniel was dead. Now, here he was, snoring.

She didn't want to move, didn't want to wake any of them. She didn't want this moment in time to pass her by. In this moment, they were all safe. In the next, who knew what would happen. It had only been a matter of weeks since she'd left the relative safety of The Property and Crossed into Away, the forbidden territory where the Others had made a sort of life for themselves. But in those few weeks, her life had changed forever, in good ways and in bad. She yearned for a few days of peace. Boring would do just fine, right about now.

She looked back at Pathik, hoping to lose herself in the shadows of his lashes again for just a little while. Instead, there were his eyes, his startling blue eyes, an inheritance from his grandfather Indigo, staring back at her. His lips curled upward and she felt herself smiling yet again.

"You okay?" Pathik spoke softly.

Rachel nodded.

Pathik sat up slowly, testing his muscles and stretching. Rachel watched him take in the sight of his family—what was left of it—and hers, relief smoothing his face. Then he stood and surveyed the dry beach they had dragged themselves up onto. He assessed the meager supplies they had managed to drag up the beach, safe from the tide's hungry grasp. Finally, his gaze lingered on Nandy, the only mother he had ever known.

"Nipper?" Pathik whispered the question.

Rachel shook her head. "No sign of him." She'd been scanning the beach for the Woolly since she awoke, hoping to see him. The look on Nandy's face the night before when the storm had ripped him out of the boat had been heartbreaking. Rachel had to admit she'd developed a soft spot for the strange creature herself. He was fierce, a mixture of feline muscle and woolly-furred *something*, with razor-sharp claws and, to put it politely, an independent nature. But he'd helped Rachel find her father when nobody else could. And he was Nandy's special friend. Not a pet—there was no way anyone could call Nipper a pet—but he *was* a very special friend.

"Shall we go look for him, and get an idea of where we are?" Pathik still spoke quietly.

"We can't leave them asleep and unguarded."

Pathik grinned and nodded toward Malgam. Rachel looked and saw that his eyes were open. She wondered how long he'd been awake. She hoped he hadn't been observing her while she watched Pathik sleeping.

"I'll keep an eye out," Malgam said. "But don't go far. And get back here soon." Even after being half-drowned, Malgam still managed to sound prickly.

Pathik walked over to where Malgam lay and knelt, silently touching his shoulder. Then he rose and went to Rachel's side.

"Let's go."

After one long look at her parents, who were still sleeping, Rachel followed. The two of them headed inland, toward a stand of wind-twisted evergreen trees on a bluff above the beach they had staggered onto, bedraggled and wet, the night before.

"Do you think Nipper made it ashore?" Rachel thought of the waves, taller than their boat, powerful enough to kill all of them easily. She could still feel them reaching for her, eager to snatch her up whole and devour her.

Pathik said nothing for a moment. Then he shrugged. "*We* made it to shore. Maybe he did, too."

The morning sun was gaining strength and Rachel felt her shoulder muscles relax as its warmth caressed them. When they reached the bluff, Pathik stopped and cast his head back and forth in that odd way he had, trying to sense anything emanating from within the stand of trees. Rachel couldn't help grinning. When he used his gift he looked like a dog, sniffing the air for a scent. Pathik was searching for feelings, as his gift allowed him to, feelings that would alert him to the presence of any strangers and what their state of mind might be. He described it as feeling for different colors, each associated with different emotions.

"Anything?" Rachel didn't tease him like she usually did.

Pathik shook his head. "I don't get a thing." He narrowed his eyes at the copse, as though he might see something there that his other senses didn't reveal.

Rachel didn't know whether to feel disappointed or relieved that Pathik didn't sense anyone in the trees. She was thankful they'd made it to Salishan, but there was something foreboding about the island, despite the sun shining bright in the sky. She couldn't name what it was that made her feel this way, but it was strong.

Indigo had been certain that there were people here, even though the island had been evacuated decades ago because it was too expensive to include it in the Border Defense System. Rachel wondered what effect Korusal's bombs, dropped all those years ago, had on Salishan. Were there animals here like there were Away? Savage baerns, capable of ripping a person apart? If there were people, did they have strange gifts like the Others, who had barely survived when Away was hit?

They moved slowly into the copse, eyeing the distorted branches, twisted by the sea winds until they resembled outstretched arms clutching for whatever came into range. Pathik took the lead, and this time Rachel let him without protest. They made their way across ground cushioned by years of dead needles, through which no undergrowth could grow. It was a change from the forests Away, where the undergrowth made travel more difficult. This was almost like walking through a park, somewhere on the Unified State's side of the Line.

There were no signs of people—not at first. There was just the oddly silent copse, deeply carpeted with needles from the twisted trees. They moved slowly, cautiously, uncertain of what might be just ahead, just out of sight. When Pathik stopped, Rachel, who had been checking behind them, ran right into him.

"Your trekking skills still need some work." Pathik grinned.

"I can't help it if you decide to stop for no reason, with no warning." Rachel didn't feel as irritated as she sometimes did with Pathik; the fact that she could have lost him last night in the sea was still with her. She didn't know if she could ever forget his cold, lifeless body on the beach, how frantic she'd felt when she realized he wasn't breathing.

They kept walking, stopping now and then to let Pathik sniff, listening carefully for any sounds that might betray someone's—or some *thing's*—approach. Rachel couldn't see anything but the twisted trees ahead. When she looked behind them again, she couldn't see the beach anymore. They'd gone further than they planned. She was just about to say something to Pathik when he stopped, held his hand up without looking back at her.

She stopped too, and waited, silent. But when he said nothing, she walked up to his side. He was looking ahead, down at the ground.

"What—" Rachel stopped talking when she saw what Pathik was staring at.

It was definitely blood. Blood on a path—a *manmade* path—of flat stones. The needles had been cleared here and the stones were set into the sand.

Rachel and Pathik stood studying the stain. It was fresh, but it had begun to dry in the morning sun, leaving a burnt brown glaze on the flat stones that formed the path.

"Seems like a lot," said Pathik.

Rachel nodded. Then she noticed something along the edge of the blood stain—something that made her feel sick. "Look, Pathik."

It was a smudged foot print—a *paw* print. Rachel hoped she was wrong, but Pathik's whisper confirmed her fears.

"Nipper." Woolly prints were unique enough that Pathik had no doubts.

Rachel heard the pain in his voice and knew he was thinking of Nandy. When they agreed to seek refuge on Salishan, the hardest part for Nandy had been leaving Nipper behind. She'd raised the Woolly from a cub and grown to love him, but she knew the journey would be dangerous. Nipper had other ideas, though. He'd made his own decision on the day they left Away, by hopping into the boat they would use to get to the island and refusing to get out.

"He made it to shore," said Pathik. He thought

about the night before: about the wave that washed Nipper from the boat, about the boat capsizing. They were all so very lucky. He reached out and took Rachel's hand.

"He could just be injured." Rachel tried not to think about what the bloody print might mean.

"Whatever could injure Nipper enough to cause that much blood . . ." Pathik shook his head. "We'd better get back to the others. We'll need to find a safer place to camp—something less exposed." They'd all been so exhausted the night before that they had dragged themselves up the beach a bit and called it good. But it appeared that there were things to hide from on Salishan.

"Maybe there are Woollies here, too, just like Away. Maybe that print belongs to one of *them*." Rachel sounded like she was trying to convince herself.

"Maybe." Pathik drew her toward him and held her for a moment. There had been too much death already. "Let's go back." He turned to go, but he only got one step.

Rachel didn't understand what was happening at first. She thought maybe Pathik was playing, trying to make her bump into him again so he could tease her about her trekking skills. He just . . . fell. One moment he was turning, walking, the next he was slumped on the ground. She knelt next to him, felt his pulse. He was breathing. She ran her hands over his body—neck, arms, chest—and couldn't find any injury.

That was all she had time to do.

There were four of them: two men and two women. They were standing a few feet away, watching Rachel. Instinctively, she tried to cover Pathik's body with her own, to shield him from whatever might come.

"What did you do to him?" Rachel couldn't stop her voice from shaking.

"He's fine," said one of the women. She raised her eyebrows at one of the men. "Right, Jim?"

The man she addressed scowled at her, but made no reply. She turned to the second man. "Well? What do they have?"

The man dropped his gaze to Pathik. "He has something, but not strong enough to worry about." He looked at Rachel. "She's got *nothing*. I say we take her along home, find out if she's a stray or what."

Rachel didn't have to hear more—she opened her mouth and started screaming.

For about two seconds.

The sound just stopped. Her mouth was still wide open, her lungs still pushing air out, but the *sound* of her scream cut off almost immediately. She tried again, taking another huge gulp of air and screaming as loud as she could—nothing. She saw that the other woman, the one who hadn't said anything yet, had her eyes closed, concentrating. She had the strangest feeling the woman could somehow see her anyway, that she was looking straight at her.

Things happened fast. The two men started toward her. Pathik groaned, seemed to be coming back to consciousness, but fell limp again. The women just stood, one watching, the other one with her eyes still closed. Rachel scrambled to her feet, too late, and the men grabbed her arms.

"How long will he be out?" The woman directed the question to the man she called Jim.

"Half hour, at least." Jim tightened his grip on Rachel's arm. "Stop thrashing around. Won't do you any good."

She didn't stop though. She fought as hard as she could, pulling one way and then another, trying to slip herself free. She kept screaming too, though it didn't matter. It was one of the most frightening sensations she'd ever experienced—screaming and screaming, unable to make a sound.

They kept hold of her, but they couldn't do much else. The second man spoke.

"She's too wild. We won't get far with her like this. Not fast enough, anyway."

The first woman, who seemed to be the one in charge, considered. "You're right, David. Better she doesn't see the way, too." The woman looked at Jim. "I know it's two, but I can amp it for you. We won't have to doze him for long, anyway—just until we're gone."

Jim nodded, looked down at Pathik for a moment, then fixed his gaze on Rachel.

Everything went black.

Chapter 2

We've got to go *now*!" Pathik was bent over with his hands on his knees, trying to catch his breath. Malgam, who had been the only one awake when Pathik ran back into camp, had already checked him for injuries. Vivian, Daniel, and Nandy were gathered around, trying to understand what had happened.

"*Who* took her? What do you mean they—" Vivian couldn't continue. The idea that Rachel was gone—again—lost to her when she'd just got her family back together, was too much. She swayed on her feet, allowing Daniel to hold her steady.

"I don't know who took her." Pain and anger shone out like hard lights from Pathik's eyes. "I never saw them. All I know is one minute I was walking and the next I was unconscious. When I came to, Rachel was gone."

"You never *felt* them, either?" Malgam frowned. "You checked, right?"

Pathik's eyes widened as he realized the implications of Malgam's question. "I did check. There was nothing. And if they were anywhere near us, I would have picked up on them unless—"

"Unless they had some way to block you. Block your gift with one of their own." Daniel looked worried. "Sounds like they don't practice Usage here."

"So we know there are people, we know they have gifts—at least one—and there's no reason to think they don't have others, just like we do. And now we know they have no qualms using them on others." Nandy sighed. "Not the best scenario."

Malgam nodded. "Indigo always said without Usage we were lost. Too many ways to hurt each other without rules."

"We need to go find Rachel." Vivian had recovered herself enough to be impatient with all the discussion. "Now."

Daniel nodded. "You and Malgam move camp—someplace with more cover, further into the trees there." He held up a hand at Malgam's expression—he didn't look pleased at being relegated to camp detail. "You're still not back to a hundred percent Malgam. Better if Pathik, Nandy and I go right now."

"You're not exactly back to normal either, Daniel." Malgam scowled at his friend. Both men had recently suffered physically—Daniel from being captured and tortured by the Roberts, Malgam from being gravely ill. The journey to Salishan hadn't been all that easy either.

Vivian was already gathering their things. "Malgam, come on. We're wasting time." She shook out one of the blankets they'd managed to dry out and folded it, as if the faster she moved the sooner she might see Rachel again.

Nandy grabbed one of the water containers and shook it. From the sloshing she heard she judged it to be about half full. "We'll take this one." She went to Malgam and hugged him. "Be careful."

"*You* be careful," he said, hugging her back. "I'll be watching, if you don't mind."

Nandy smiled. "I don't mind at all, but I think you'd better conserve your strength. Using your gift right now might not be the best thing. We might need you later."

Malgam frowned. His gift was sight—he could see, with great effort, through the eyes of others—at least others he knew well. He wanted to argue, but he knew Nandy was right. He was still weak.

Daniel interrupted Vivian's mad scramble to pack up camp by taking hold of her shoulders. "We'll find her," he whispered into her ear. He could feel the tightness in her; he knew how afraid she must be for their daughter. He was just as afraid.

"Bring her back." Vivian looked into his eyes—this man she'd thought was dead for so many years, standing right in front of her. It still felt like some sort of miracle to her.

Pathik had been watching the farewells impatiently. "Let's go," he said, checking that his knife was secure in his leg sheath. He turned and started walking the way he and Rachel had gone when they left camp.

Nandy fell in behind him. Daniel squeezed Vivian's shoulders one more time and joined the two. Malgam and Vivian watched them walk away, watched until they disappeared over a bluff. Then Malgam turned to her.

"They'll bring her back," he said, his voice rough. "Nandy said I could check in, so once we have the camp moved I may need you to keep watch while I do." He didn't mention that Nandy had said *not* to check in.

"Daniel told me about that. Your gift." She hesitated. "Is it considered rude to ask about it?"

Malgam laughed. "I never thought about that. We just all knew about them, Away. By the time you were five, if you had one, everyone in camp knew what it was." He knelt, stuffed some of the clothes they had laid out to dry into a duffle bag. "It's not rude."

Vivian studied him. "You were a big part of Daniel being rescued from the Roberts—you and your gift. He said if you hadn't been able to see what he was seeing, he never would have been found."

Malgam grunted. "Me and Nandy's spoiled old Woolly. He was as big a part of it as I was." Malgam kept hoping Nipper would appear. He had no special affection for the thing, but he did love Nandy and she was inconsolable at the thought that Nipper had drowned.

"So that's what it is, though? You just—see what another person is looking at?" Vivian still didn't understand how the Others were able to do the things they did—she knew it was some sort of genetic mutation from the bombs. Daniel had told her the Others didn't fully understand the gifts, themselves.

Malgam scanned the beach, looking for anything else that might have washed ashore from their boat. "That's what it is." He stood. "Only through the eyes of those I know, though, and know pretty well." Talking about it made him remember his father, Indigo. It made him see those last moments of his father's life again, moments he wished with all his being he could change. "I think we'd better get going."

Vivian nodded. She looked around. "Not much to move, is there?"

"I know. We're going to have to find water soon, and hope there's some sort of food here." Malgam shrugged. "Maybe some more of our things will show up on the beach."

They started moving inland.

"I forgot about that." Pathik stared at the blood, wincing. Nandy had cried out when she saw the paw print. "I'm sorry, Nandy. That's what we were looking at when they took Rachel."

Nandy knelt, touched the dried blood. "Too much of it to think he's still alive." She stood again. "He made it to shore through that storm, just to have someone . . ." She set her jaw and turned away from the blood.

"You don't remember anything? Not where they stood, how many there were?" Daniel looked around, seeking any sort of clue to what happened to Rachel.

"Nothing. Like I said, I just blacked out." Pathik nudged one of the flat stones that made up the path; it had been dislodged from the sand. "She put up a fight, judging from this."

"Here." Nandy had walked a few feet away. She pointed to the ground. "There were at least two. A man and a woman. Maybe more."

Daniel and Pathik joined her and stared at the footprints in the sand. They were indistinct, but it was clear that some were much larger and made by someone heavier than the others.

"They headed that way." Pathik looked in the direction the prints led. Without another word he started walking, slowly, studying the ground.

Nandy and Daniel exchanged a look.

"He's not going to be easy to hold down if he finds them," said Nandy. "He's blaming himself." She hesitated. "And he loves her."

Daniel nodded. "I know he does. And he shouldn't blame himself. But I have to say, I'm not going to be easy to hold down either, if they've harmed her." He started after Pathik.

Nandy watched the two of them for a moment before she followed. "Let's hope they haven't hurt her," she whispered.

The trail was scant—a half footprint here and there, not even really prints, because once they left the sand around the stone path, tree needles blanketed everything like carpet. They found places where feet had disturbed the needles slightly and followed. It was quiet now that they were out of earshot of the shore. The only sounds came from some sort of birds trilling high above them in the trees. After what seemed like forever to Pathik, they emerged from the trees onto open ground. A rocky field stretched before them and beyond it, craggy foothills turned into a distant mountain of stone.

"How big *is* this island?" Daniel shaded his eyes from the sun with one hand. He scanned the rough field, hoping to see some movement, some sign of Rachel.

"Indigo never said—I doubt he knew. We didn't have good records, either." Nandy tried to calculate how far the mountain was from where they stood.

"Do you see that—is that a trail? To the right of that big rock there?" Daniel pointed at a faint line far off in the foot hills. It meandered up toward the mountain, too regular to be completely natural.

Nandy nodded. "It has to be." She squinted. "But it seems to end, just there—see? Like a path to nowhere. They couldn't have taken her there, could they?"

"We have to go find out." Pathik started forward again, but Nandy called him back.

"Pathik, we need to stay together. This looks like it's going to be more of a trek than a day trip. We need to go back, get Vivian and Malgam, find some water. That path will take us the rest of the day to reach."

Pathik started to protest, but he knew Nandy was right. Still, all he could think about was Rachel, being taken further and further away. "Let's move it." He turned and headed back the way they had come, moving quickly.

Nandy watched him go. She shrugged at Daniel. "I guess we'd better step it up."

They found Vivian and Malgam up the bluff from the beach. Malgam had made three trips back and forth from the shoreline to the new campsite with various items from their boat—they *had* washed ashore, at least some of them. There were twelve precious water containers in one pack, some more bags of clothes, the water-proofed bag that contained Vivian's portfolio and other documents, more freeze-dried food packs. Vivian had nearly cried when she saw the orchid cubes that Rachel had carefully packed—they were a mess. Seawater had made its way inside each of them. All the orchid crosses Ms. Moore had helped Rachel prepare for the journey when they were still on The Property were dead.

They took some time to eat, all of them but Pathik. He stood a few feet away from them, impatiently watching. Then they organized all the supplies into several packs so that they could each carry one or two. It was afternoon when they started out, but nobody even hinted at waiting for the next morning; they knew they had to stay as close behind whomever had taken Rachel as they could. Daniel and Nandy filled Vivian and Malgam in on what they'd found as they walked. Pathik was silent, walking ahead of the rest.

"I'm worried about him." Vivian spoke to Nandy in a low voice, nodding toward Pathik. "He's just over blaming himself for his grandfather's death, and now he's convinced Rachel getting taken is his fault, too."

Nandy kept walking, her eyes on the ground. "Do *you* blame him?"

"Blamc Pathik?" Vivian sounded surprised. "Why would I?"

Nandy shrugged. "He let her go with him, let her scout when she could have stayed at the camp, with you."

Vivian snorted. "*Let* her? Like she *let* him go into Bensen?" She was silent for a moment, remembering the awful cost of that thrill-seeking trip Pathik and Rachel had made to Bensen. Indigo had paid for it with his life. But she shook her head at the thought that anyone could be blamed for it—that was wrong, really. Indigo, Pathik, Rachel—all of them—they all had choices to make. She looked sideways at Nandy. "Do you really think either one of them could stop the other from doing whatever they set their minds to?"

Nandy smiled. "Probably not. No more than

Malgam could stop me—or Daniel, you?"

"Exactly." Vivian shook her head. "I'd like to blame *someone*, but it wouldn't help anything. Rachel would still be gone." She eyed the rocky field, the foothills ahead. She tried not to think about what might be happening to Rachel.

It was after dusk when they finally stopped for the night. They'd made it to the first of the foothills and located a carefully hidden trailhead. Pathik sniffed around, trying to determine if anyone was near.

"They'll just block you, if they're still close." Malgam put a hand on Pathik's shoulder. "Come get some food now."

Pathik followed him to where the rest of the group had set up a makeshift camp. The plan was to eat, sleep a few hours, and be back to hiking before dawn.

"I don't think we can be that far behind," said Nandy, trying to ease Pathik's mind a bit. "They'll be either leading her or carrying her and that will slow them down."

"Why would . . . whoever they are . . . take Rachel and not Pathik?" Vivian chewed on a piece of freeze-dried meat, tasting nothing. She swallowed and took another bite. She wasn't hungry at all—her stomach was tight with worry for her daughter—but she knew she might need every bit of strength the meal provided. "And how did they even know we were here?"

"If they can block a gift like Pathik's, they probably have people with the same gift, or something like it." Daniel untied a bedroll. "They probably knew about us the minute we got here."

Pathik stood. "I'll take first watch." He stared through the growing dark at the trailhead, or at least at the place he knew it was—they'd barely been able to identify it in daylight. Someone had taken great care to ensure that the trail wasn't easy to see, that it looked like no more than an animal path. He wanted nothing more than to follow it, now, and find Rachel, but he knew the others were right. They had no idea what they'd be walking into. Best to have strength in numbers.

The others settled into fitful sleep. Pathik leaned against a rock outcropping, as still as though he was made of stone, too. He listened, straining to hear anything that might warn him of danger. He *felt*, too, trying to see if he could sense a block. He hadn't known he was being blocked that morning, so he hadn't tried to sense anything different, but now, he did. He concentrated, casting out with his mind, feeling for anything unusual. He didn't feel any human presence, but just as he was about to stop, he did feel—something. It was like a veil, a soft black wall, past which everything was obscured. As soon as he felt it, he withdrew.

He didn't know if it was possible for whoever was casting that veil to sense him, here in the dark, reaching out to feel them, but he didn't want to take the chance. He stared up, into the murky blackness of the mountain, mammoth against the night sky. Rachel was there, somewhere. Alive. He had to believe that.

Chapter 3

The winter sun shone dimly through the roof of the greenhouse, its tepid evening rays magnified by the glass panes. Elizabeth took the last pot from the tray of orchids she was working on. Repotting was an endless task, but she'd made good progress today. Just one more plant and then she would walk to the main house, where Jonathan, who'd moved into one of the guest bedrooms, would certainly be making some catastrophe for dinner.

She had to smile, thinking of how bad he was at cooking. He'd been so kind, though, tried so hard to see to her needs since Vivian and Rachel had left,

Crossing the Line to who knew where.

Crossing the Line. Like she should have done, all those years ago, with Indigo and her baby son. She still felt the shame of her cowardice, even now, when it made no difference at all. Indigo was dead, her son was Away. Her grandson, too. At least she'd been able to meet Pathik, brief as that acquaintance had been. He was a bright boy, made of good stuff, she could tell, even in the short time she'd had with him. She wondered if his father, Malgam, was like him. Malgam, her son.

"Just about finished?" Jonathan stood in the greenhouse doorway. His ever-present hat was tilted down over his wrinkled forehead, tufts of gray hair peeking out from the brim.

"Yes." Elizabeth trimmed the dried roots of the plant she held, careful to stop just short of viable tissue. She popped the orchid back into the pot, tamping potting mixture around it gently.

"Hope you're hungry." Jonathan grinned. "I think tonight is my best dish yet."

Elizabeth didn't look up. "I'll be along directly."

"I'll wait. Looks like you're almost done, and it's getting dark out." Jonathan leaned against the door frame. He glanced toward the main road, looking for lights.

"I don't think they'll be back tonight." Elizabeth shook her head. "Surely once today is enough, even for them."

The Enforcement Officers had been by earlier, as they had every day since Vivian, Rachel and the rest had Crossed. They knew something was suspect about Elizabeth's story—they weren't buying that her household employee had just disappeared, especially not so soon after that very employee's daughter had been reported missing under strange circumstances. Elizabeth did her best to ignore the EO's vehicle as it drove slowly down the long driveway to The Property each day. She was grateful they didn't stop and question her. She knew that luck wouldn't last.

"Still, better safe than sorry." Jonathan didn't move from his place in the doorway.

"Have it your way." Elizabeth checked the timer on the misters and cleaned her tools. When she was satisfied that all was as it should be, she joined Jonathan. They walked the short path to the main house, sharing a companionable silence. Jonathan opened the back kitchen door for her; they'd stopped using the grand front doors much.

"Smells . . . good?" Elizabeth couldn't keep the surprise from her voice.

Jonathan shot her a look. "Like I said, my best yet." He bustled around the kitchen, lifting the lid from a pot, letting fragrant steam escape.

"Shall I set the table when I've washed up?" Elizabeth started for the hall bathroom.

"All set. You could pour the wine, though."

The table was set for the two of them—a sad little sight, Elizabeth thought, looking at the empty chairs, remembering the grand dinner parties her mother and father used to have. That seemed a century ago, though. So many things had changed. She poured them each a glass of wine, and sniffed appreciatively when Jonathan brought in the main dish. It was pasta of some sort, with a sauce that actually smelled delicious.

"What's the occasion?" Elizabeth gestured toward the wine bottle. They didn't usually have wine with dinner.

Jonathan held up a hand. "Let me get this dished out, first." He scooped up some pasta with tongs and placed it on Elizabeth's plate. Then he ladled a sauce over the pasta and added some freshly ground pepper.

The front doorbell chimed.

Elizabeth and Jonathan exchanged a glance.

"Who?" Jonathan whispered the word.

"No one good." Elizabeth stood. She placed her napkin—a fine linen napkin from her mother's supply—on the table next to her plate. "Let me handle it."

Jonathan set the saucepan down carefully, making sure it was squarely on the trivet which protected the fine wood table. "I'll come with you."

"I said *let me handle it*." Elizabeth immediately regretted her tone. So many years of rebuffing Jonathan had become habit. Still, they both knew that someone at the door this late couldn't be bringing welcomed news. And Elizabeth didn't want Jonathan put at any more risk than he already had been.

Jonathan remained standing. "Go on, then." He didn't look at her.

Elizabeth tried to soften her tone. "I'll just tell them we're at dinner." She moved toward the front doors slowly, dread in each step. When she reached them she pressed the intercom button. "Yes?"

"Elizabeth Moore?" The voice was a man's, brusque and official.

"Yes."

"I'm here to interview you regarding a Vivian Quillen. Open the door, please."

Elizabeth did. The man waiting wore a typical government suit: dark jacket, dark pants, dark shoes. He carried a slim briefcase and looked impatient. "This won't take long." He pushed past Elizabeth and into the foyer.

She turned to face him, slowly. "We," she said, carefully enunciating each word, "have just begun to dine."

"I guess that will have to wait." The man was unimpressed with Elizabeth's frostiness. "I need to get some information from you, Ms. Moore. Where shall we have our little talk?"

"What did you say your name was?" Elizabeth kept the ice in her voice.

"I didn't say." The man flashed an identification card and raised his eyebrows over cold, gray eyes. "I don't have time to waste here, Ms. Moore."

Elizabeth wanted to tell him exactly what she thought of him, wanted to show him the door and go back to the dining room where Jonathan waited with his pasta. But she knew she couldn't. The fact that this man was on her doorstep, the fact that he wasn't just some EO, cruising by the house, giving her some stupid grin from the vehicle, told her she needed to be careful. "We can talk in the parlor."

She turned without waiting to see if he followed, and settled herself in one of the chairs flanking the fireplace.

"Now." The man set his briefcase on the low table between them and opened it. He took out a digitab and scanned the screen for a moment, flicking his finger back and forth. Without looking up, he spoke.

"It says here that your employee, one Vivian Quillen, is missing." He frowned at the screen. "And that her daughter was reported missing as well, sometime before Ms. Quillen." The man finally raised his eyes, peering at Elizabeth over his digitab. "It says you weren't too cooperative in your initial interview, Ms. Moore." He leaned back against the chair, crossed his legs and watched her.

Elizabeth said nothing. She heard a sound out in the foyer and knew Jonathan had stationed himself outside the parlor door.

"Well?" The man uncrossed his legs. He leaned forward, lowering the digitab. "As I said, I don't have time to waste here. I'm sure you know it's in your best interest to cooperate with me." He looked disdainfully around the room. "You wouldn't want to have to leave all this . . . luxury."

"I have no plans to leave." Elizabeth followed his gaze with her own, taking in all of the memories the room held. Her mother's favorite glass box sat on the mantle, right next to the digim of Indigo. It was an image of him in his youth, blue eyes, ready smile. He'd been so handsome. He was dead now, she knew it. She'd stayed behind when the others

Crossed, both to give them some time to escape and because she'd hoped that Indigo might somehow have survived. But he'd never come back from town that day—the day he had to go rescue Pathik and Rachel. She'd been foolish to hope, she knew that, but she had. She had hoped against all reason that somehow, Indigo would return to her.

Elizabeth felt tears welling in her eyes. It took her by surprise, and she had to grit her teeth hard to stop them. She turned her gaze back to the man sitting on her mother's sofa, the despicable little man who held all the power he needed to have her hauled away to some cell, even killed.

He was waiting for her attention. "You," he said, grinning, "don't make the plans." The grin transformed into a set of bared teeth, framed by his thin, hard lips. "*We* make the plans." He waited until he was certain she'd taken his point. "Your former employee, this Ms. Quillen, has an interesting history." He checked his digitab again. "From what I see here, you indicated in a previous interview that you had no idea she was a collaborator."

"Of course I had no idea, and I don't think it's been established that she was one." Elizabeth tried to look as affronted as possible. "I would never hire a collaborator. Why would I bring that kind of trouble to an already troubled business? I've been barely able to pay your taxes for years. Costs are up, sales are down—"

"I'm not interested in your personal problems." The man breathed in through his nose, the sound like the hissing of a snake. "We're watching you, as

I'm sure you know, Ms. Moore. We plan to keep watching you. It would be better for you if you just tell us what you know now, instead of waiting until we discover it on our own. Things could go very badly for you then. For you, and for anyone else who might be involved." He turned his head slightly toward the foyer, but he kept his eyes on her, and smiled. "It seems your hired man has taken up residence here, of late. Rather a cozy arrangement. It would be a shame if he somehow became involved in your mess, wouldn't it?"

"I've told your people everything I know about that woman and her daughter." Elizabeth let the tears she'd been hiding show. "I don't know what else you want from me. I've always tried to be a good citizen—my family has served, as I'm sure you're aware—in high places. I don't know anything about that woman, other than that she was in need when I employed her and she brought no trouble here for many years."

The man studied Elizabeth, gauging her display of emotion. He seemed unconvinced. Finally, he placed his digitab in his briefcase, snapped it shut, and stood.

"I imagine I'll be seeing you again soon, Ms. Moore." He strode toward the foyer without looking back. "Very soon."

Elizabeth hoped Jonathan had retreated back to the dining room in time. She listened to the front door click shut, and then rushed to the foyer to lock it with shaking hands. Through the peephole she watched as the man's vehicle lights faded into darkness.

"He gone?"

Elizabeth jumped. "You scared me!"

"Sorry. Just tried to stay out of your way like you said to, until the fellow left." Jonathan wore an improbable grin. "Let's go eat, shall we?"

Elizabeth smoothed her skirt. "There's nothing amusing about that man coming here. We may be in real trouble, Jonathan." She scowled at Jonathan.

"I didn't say it was amusing." Jonathan took her arm, gently. "I just said, let's eat. My best meal's getting colder every minute we dawdle out here." He led her toward the dining room. "Besides." Jonathan pulled Elizabeth's chair out for her. "We're already in trouble deep. And you know it."

Chapter 4

Rachel woke to the sound of whispers. Two people, a male and a female, she thought. She didn't move, didn't open her eyes. For a few moments she focused on keeping her breathing slow and steady, at the same time straining to hear what the whisperers were saying. It was hard to understand them—they were speaking so softly none of the words were clear.

"She's awake."

That was pretty clear.

Rachel opened her eyes. She was on a cot of some sort. Someone had taken the trouble to cover her with a light blanket made from a finely woven, soft cloth. She didn't notice that her ankle was shackled to one of the cot legs until she tried to sit up.

"Here, I'll help you." A girl with long, brown hair took her elbow.

"You could help me by untying me." Rachel tried not to let any fear into her voice. She looked around. A single candle, stuck in its own wax on a wooden crate, lit the area near her; three feet out in any direction its glow dimmed enough to make it difficult to see much. She was in a sort of alcove, in a . . . cave? A cold rock wall arched above her, disappearing into the murkiness. She could hear other people somewhere beyond the candle's light, but she couldn't see them. A curtain of what looked like layers of old fish net hung in the opening of the alcove, blocking the view.

"They won't allow that." The other whisperer—a boy, a little older than Pathik from the looks of him, sounded apologetic. "They want to be sure you're not going to cause any trouble before we untie you."

"How did you know I was awake?" Rachel thought she knew, but she wondered if they would answer her truthfully.

They didn't answer at all. The girl shrugged and looked away. The boy changed the subject.

"Are you thirsty?" He picked up a battered, but clean, tin can and offered it to her. "They said you were out the whole way back, so you probably are."

"I was *knocked* out." Rachel didn't touch the

can. "Who's in charge here?" She didn't feel as brave as she hoped she sounded.

"Jim never hurts anyone when he dozes them." The girl spoke up, sounding defensive. "Sarah wouldn't let him."

"Shut up, Hannah." The boy sounded worried.

"*You* shut up, Tom. She already knows about talent—Sarah said that boy she was with had a little."

"You're supposed to be monitoring her, not arguing." It was the woman—the woman who did all the talking while Rachel tried to scream, back at the path. She held the netting aside, stood behind Hannah and Tom looking down at Rachel. She had short brown hair and her skin shone like copper in the candlelight.

"Sorry, Sarah," Tom mumbled.

Sarah ignored Tom. "Are you planning on causing any trouble?"

Rachel glared up at her. "Where's Pathik?"

"Is that your friend?" Sarah shrugged. "He's not here, if that's what you mean. He didn't have enough talent to interest us. At least not right now."

Rachel thought of the dried blood on the stones—Nipper's blood. "If you hurt him—"

Sarah ignored her. "You, on the other hand, have *none*. No talent whatsoever. And *that* is interesting." She studied Rachel. "You're not a stray—we checked with them. So we want to know what you're doing here."

"I don't know what you're talking about." Rachel wondered what strays were. "You don't have any right to hold me here." She pointed at her ankle. "Let me loose."

Sarah shook her head. "Not just yet. We don't know anything about you, or about your friends."

Rachel was about to protest again, when an older man approached Sarah. He touched her arm, spoke low, his voice urgent. "You're needed in the office." After a nod from her, he hurried away.

"I'll be back to check on you in a bit." Sarah gave Hannah and Tom a severe look. "You two, do your jobs." Then she disappeared through the netting.

After she'd disappeared from sight, Rachel shot her own look at Hannah and Tom. "What's your job?"

The two squirmed a bit. Finally, Hannah answered Rachel's question with a question of her own. "Where did you and those others come from?"

"What others?" Rachel feigned ignorance.

Tom shook his head, grinning. "Might as well not pretend. It doesn't do you any good to hide what we already know. They counted six of you." He watched her face. "Unless there are more than that?"

Rachel sighed. "Six is right." She picked up the can of water and smelled it. It seemed okay, so she took a drink. She *was* thirsty. "How long did it take to get here from where they grabbed me?"

Hannah smiled. "We're not allowed to tell you anything, silly. You should know that."

Rachel didn't return the smile. "Why not? Will you get in trouble with her?" She nodded in the direction Sarah had gone.

"Well, yes." Tom nudged Hannah, warning her. "We would. And with . . . other people."

Rachel started working at the rope on her ankle. She ignored Tom's hushed entreaties to stop and was halfway through the first knot when Hannah knelt next to her.

"You wouldn't get far, anyway." Hannah spoke quietly. "They're not going to hurt you—they won't hurt your friends, either." She waited until Rachel stopped trying to free herself. "They just need to know who you are, why you've come. We don't get many visitors.

"Might have something to do with your hospitality." Rachel didn't feel reassured.

"She's funny." Tom grinned at Hannah, who looked back at him with an expression that was half exasperation, half affection.

"Listen, just relax, if you can." Hannah sounded sympathetic. "As soon as they figure out what's what, they'll let you loose. In the meantime, maybe some food?"

Rachel *was* hungry. She hated to admit it to this girl, though. She felt like she should be making some grand attempt to escape, to find Pathik, warn the rest of the group, but she couldn't see how.

"I could eat something."

Hannah looked pleased. "Tom, go get some food from the kitchen. I bet there's plenty—it's almost time for lunch."

"You go get it." Tom folded his arms. "I'm the one Sarah picked to watch her."

"She picked *both* of us. Besides, she's awake now, so your talent's not the one that's important. If anything happens it will be me—" Hannah stopped talking. She looked at Rachel, her eyes wide. "You *do* know about talents, right?"

Tom patted Hannah's back reassuringly. "I guess you were probably right—if her friend had some, she must know."

Rachel couldn't see the harm in being honest. "We call them gifts. But yes, I know about them."

"They say that only two in your party have any talent at all." Tom whispered the comment. "Is that really true?" He looked doubtful.

Rachel didn't answer right away. How could he—how could the people here—know that? She wondered what sort of gifts *these* people had.

"Go get the food, Tom." Hannah's eyebrows were furrowed so close they almost touched in the middle of her forehead. "You talk too much for your own good."

"You're lucky I love you." Tom scowled at Hannah, only half joking. He got up. "Ping if anything happens."

Hannah watched him go, smiling.

"What's *ping* mean?" Rachel leveled her gaze at Hannah. "Is that your gift—your talent?"

Hannah considered her for a moment. "I guess it can't really hurt to tell you." She looked over her shoulder, though, before she continued. "Pinging is my talent, yes. I can send out an alert, let someone know if you're causing trouble." She watched to see how Rachel would react. When Rachel didn't react at all, she continued. "Tom can tell if you're okay—not just you, anyone, I mean."

"Okay?" Rachel shook her head. "Okay how?"

"If you're . . . healthy, I guess. He can't diagnose things, nothing like that, but he can monitor heart rate, breathing, pulse. That sort of thing." She flipped her hair back over her shoulder. "That's why Sarah assigned us to watch you. Sort of a *while she's sleeping, once she's awake* first response team."

"Huh." Rachel tried to sound unimpressed.

Hannah noticed the coolness of her response. "Once he's back with the food and you've had something to eat, maybe Sarah will let us untie you. Maybe she'll even let us show you around a bit. You don't seem to want to cause any trouble."

"Where are we, anyway?" Rachel touched the arching wall behind her. The cold stone formed a ceiling above her. She could see where it had been worked, chiseled out to create the little alcove she and Hannah were in—it looked like some of it had been done with some crude tool. But half way up the wall, the rough carving faded into a smoother, expert sculpting. Rachel couldn't see any tool marks at all. She looked beyond the opening of the alcove, squinting to try to see through the netting. All she could make out were dots of light here and there.

"We're in the cave." Hannah said it matter-of-factly, as though there were no other place they *would* be.

Before Rachel could ask more questions, Sarah reappeared. She held the curtain aside and looked hard at Rachel. "Looks like your friends are on their way to us." She shook her head. "Pretty eager bunch."

"How could they find the cave?" Hannah sounded surprised.

Surprised, but *not* worried. That didn't make Rachel feel good.

"They haven't found it yet, but somehow they spotted the trail—the right light at the right moment." Sarah frowned. "Where's Tom?"

"He went to get her some food. He should be right back."

Sarah knelt next to Rachel and took out a knife. Before Rachel even had a chance to react, Sarah cut the rope at her ankle. She stood and shoved the knife back in the sheath that was buckled around her waist.

"You can show her around a bit, but keep a close eye on her," she said to Hannah. "If they do find an entrance, she'll be our bargaining chip. We don't want any misunderstandings." Then she left.

Hannah looked at Rachel, her eyes wide.

"What does she mean, misunderstandings?" Rachel rubbed her ankle where the rope had chafed the skin.

Hannah just shrugged. "We don't have many visitors, like I said. She doesn't know anything about you, or your friends. Like why you're here." She waited, pointedly.

Rachel didn't answer her.

Tom pushed through the netting and plopped down next to Hannah. "Here's some grub." He had a bowl of stew—some sort of meat in a thick broth. It smelled heavenly. Rachel took the bowl and started eating—she didn't stop until it was empty. When she looked up, Hannah and Tom were both staring at her, bemused expressions on their faces.

"You were a little hungry." Tom grinned.

"I was." Rachel put the bowl down on the crate. "Sarah said I could look around." She stood. "So let's go."

Hannah and Tom both scrambled to their feet.

"Hold on," Hannah took hold of Rachel's arm. "Stay close to us, and don't try anything, all right?"

"What would I try?" Rachel shook Hannah's hand away. She pulled the netting curtain aside and stepped out of the alcove, Hannah and Tom right behind her.

They *were* in a cave. It was immense, larger than Ms. Moore's whole house back on The Property. Rachel couldn't see the ceiling, just rocky walls that rose high up above her. The dots of light she had seen earlier through the netting were oil lamps, set along the cave's walls in nooks and crannies, casting a flickering glow. People—lots of people—were gathered in small groups, some talking, some working at various tasks. All those nearest the alcove turned and stared when Rachel emerged.

"They're just curious." Hannah waved at a girl who was sitting nearby, sharpening a knife. The girl stared at Rachel, all the while drawing a sharpening stone along the blade of the knife she held. She didn't wave back.

"She's *so* dramatic," Hannah whispered. "Let's do the tour." She and Tom started walking away from where the girl sat. Rachel held the staring girl's gaze for a moment, then followed.

"This," Hannah made a gesture that encompassed the whole of the cave, "is the common area. We all gather here to work at inside tasks, or have meetings, or eat."

Rachel nodded, scanning the enormous room. There were different areas set up in the space. Some were small, like the one where the girl was sharpening knives. It only had a work table and a couple of chairs. There was a larger area set up with many benches, which reminded Rachel of the council room Away. She could see yet another that looked like it might be for people to eat in; there were tables and benches enough to seat at least fifty.

Rachel noticed Tom's knife, hanging from a belt around his waist; she saw Hannah had one, too. They were like the knife Sarah had used to cut the rope from her ankle; not crude, hand-made blades like the ones Away. She remembered how scarce knives had been there and wondered if all of the people here had weapons. "How many of you are there?"

"There are around—"

"Enough." Hannah cut Tom off. She glared at him for a moment before she turned to Rachel. "Look. We're not supposed to tell you anything much. At least not yet. It's nothing personal."

"Nothing personal? You attack me and Pathik, you abduct me and bring me here and tie me to a cot and—"

"Nobody attacked you, did they?" Hannah looked genuinely worried.

"What do you call using gifts against people?" Rachel spat the words.

"Jim just dozed you." Tom stepped up, as though he thought Rachel might strike Hannah. "That's not attacking you. It doesn't even hurt."

"I was taken against my will. And what did they do to Pathik?" Rachel narrowed her eyes at Tom. "You people don't have Usage, do you?"

"What's Usage?"

The thought of Pathik made Rachel stop talking. She felt like if she spoke another word she would either cry or scream, right then. Hannah had said they hadn't hurt him, wouldn't hurt any of them, but Rachel didn't trust it. These people didn't even practice Usage. People with no rules about how they could use their gifts might do anything.

A scream sounded then in the dim cavern. A long, angry scream, echoing off the rock walls.

Chapter 5

The trail led them treacherously up the mountainside, crumbling rock and switchbacks making the journey difficult. Once, Vivian lost her footing and nearly fell off the disintegrating edge, but Daniel caught her hand and hauled her back up, scraped and bruised. When they finally reached the place where, from below, it had appeared that the trail just vanished, the terrain told a slightly different tale.

The main trail *did* end, but there were signs—a scrubby bush with a broken branch, an area of compacted dirt among the stones—that revealed where others had traveled. Still, that scant path didn't take them anywhere much before it disappeared as well. Even Nandy, a fairly expert tracker, had no suggestions. She headed back the way they'd come to see if she had missed anything.

The others used the time to rest. Malgam took the water bottle from his pack and drank from it. He watched his son pace back and forth in the tiny area available, then capped the bottle and tossed it to him. "We'll figure it out," he said.

Pathik caught the bottle and drank, too. "I don't understand. They had to bring her this way—the prints halfway up were definitely theirs. But to where?"

Daniel looked as frustrated as Pathik. "Maybe if we push on, there'll be more signs ahead." He took the water bottle Vivian held out to him.

"I think we're looking in the wrong place." Nandy was back, a sly grin on her face.

"You found something." Pathik smiled, too. He felt hope for the first time since Rachel had been taken.

"Back there, about fifty feet." Nandy took the water bottle Malgam offered her. She gulped from it, wiping perspiration from her forehead with her other hand. "This," she pointed at the faint signs they had followed to a dead end, "is nothing but a ruse. They made it look like they were hiding the rest of the trail, but the entrance is really back there." Nandy tilted her head back the way they had come.

"The entrance?" Vivian frowned. "The

entrance to what?"

Nandy shouldered the pack she'd left on the ground when she left to backtrack. "The entrance to the mountain."

"See?" Nandy pointed to a mass of scrub brush, just off the trail. They'd passed many just like it on the way up the mountain. This one looked no different, upon first inspection.

Pathik stepped up to the shrubs and peered down, looking for whatever it was Nandy had seen. "What about it? Just looks like a bunch of dead bushes to me."

"Exactly." Daniel stepped up next to Pathik. He touched one of the leaves; it broke off in his fingers. "They're dead. Those," Daniel pointed back down the trail at another clump of bushes, "are alive." He tugged at the branch. The whole thing came loose, revealing a cut end with twine wrapped around it.

Pathik grabbed a branch and pulled. It, too, came away easily. Soon, with all of them working, the whole clump of what had looked like bushes was strewn at their feet—all cut branches that had been tied into place.

"Look." Vivian whispered the word, as though someone they didn't want to might hear. She was staring at a trap door, made of old, dry wood, covered now with a scattering of dry leaves from the branches they had removed.

"A hatch." Malgam bent over and picked up the metal ring set into the heavy wooden door. He turned and looked up at his companions. "Here we go."

"Wait." It was Nandy. She unsheathed her knife—an ancient, pitted thing with a handle that had been repaired countless times. She readied it to strike and nodded to Malgam. "Now."

Malgam pulled, finally taking hold of the ring with both hands in order to lift the door. Daniel helped him lift it up off the frame it was set into, and the two of them leaned it against the rocks behind it. There was a gaping hole in the stone at their feet. The wood frame that had held the door was obviously hand-made and very old.

"Stairs." Pathik started to enter the hole the hatch had covered, but Malgam took his arm.

"Not so fast, Pathik." Malgam squinted into the hole. "We don't know what we're getting into here."

"We're getting Rachel back." Pathik jutted his chin out. "That's all we need to know."

"Pathik." Vivian stepped closer to him. "I want Rachel back just as much as you do, but we need to think about this, make a plan. Whatever's down there—"

"Rachel's down there." Pathik said the words evenly. He put a foot on the first step, then turned back to Vivian. "And the plan is we get her back." With that, he began to descend the steps.

Vivian and the others exchanged glances. Finally Daniel smiled and shook his head. "Well, he's right, really. We already know we're probably up against more than we can handle, but that's not stopping me from going after her, either."

"Let's go, then." Vivian stepped in front of Daniel and started down the stairs after Pathik.

It was dark, darker the deeper they went. The stairs were solid, built long ago but built sturdily. There were cobwebs here and there, but not many.

"Used fairly often, I'd say." Malgam slid his hand along the rock wall. "Doesn't look like this was formed naturally, but it wasn't chipped out by hand, either."

"Could they possibly have power here?" Daniel examined the wall, too. "It looks almost too fine for a drill, though."

The steps descended at a steep angle and ended at a small, stone landing. From there, two tunnels extended, one to the west and one to the north, black holes that gave no clues.

"Which do you think?" Nandy didn't look too happy about either option.

Before anyone could answer, three men emerged from the depths of the west tunnel. Nandy drew her knife and turned toward them, joined quickly by Malgam. When Daniel and Vivian added their blades to the show of force, the men just stood watching, unimpressed.

A sound at the north tunnel entrance explained their lack of concern. Five more people emerged—three women and two men. Each held a knife or a club.

Pathik hadn't drawn his knife. He stood with his hands held out to his sides, palms open. "Just let her go." Pathik took a step toward the men in the west tunnel. The one in front, a man about the same age as Malgam and Daniel, cocked his head.

"At least this one has some sense." He looked past Pathik at the rest of the group. "In case you hadn't noticed, you're at a distinct disadvantage." The man nodded toward the other tunnel.

"We don't want any trouble." Daniel lowered his knife. "We just want our girl back."

"Why are you here?" The question came from one of the women. She was tall, as tall as any of the men and she held a knife, low in front of her like a fighter.

"We came because we heard this place was safe." Nandy scowled at the woman. "Obviously we were wrong."

"Came from where?" The woman kept the blade of her knife pointed right at Nandy.

"Away." Pathik stepped closer to Nandy. "We came from Away."

"We're not playing here." The woman shot Pathik a look that clearly expressed her impatience.

"Neither are we." Pathik sounded angry. "Where's Rachel?"

"When you answer some questions we might be able to talk about that, boy."

"I've answered your question. Now where is Rachel?" Pathik bristled, ready to spring at the woman.

It was Daniel who finally understood the problem. He put his arm out in front of Pathik, who looked ready to fight. "He *did* answer. We came from a place called Away—that's what they . . . what *we* know it as. It might be more familiar to you by another name, depending on what history you still know. It's on the mainland, part of the area that was left out when the bombs hit."

The man considered that information. He caught the woman's eye across the landing and something imperceptible passed between them. "Like us. Left outside the boundaries, like no more than garbage." The man nodded. "But why come here?"

"We heard it was a place where we might be able to live without . . ." Daniel shrugged, at a loss to explain.

"There were people Away, people who wanted to run things in ways we didn't." Malgam watched the man absorb his answer. "There was another group, too, that made trouble for us."

The man stared at Malgam for a long time.

"You know I'm speaking truth," said Malgam. "You're reading me."

For a split-second, the man looked surprised. Then he grinned. "So you *do* know about talent." He raised his eyebrows at his companions. "It was detected in only two of you, and weak talent at that. *Everyone* here has talent. Made us wonder who you might be—if you meant us any harm. We've seen trouble before, from people with no talent."

"Talent?" Vivian looked to Daniel, to see if he understood what the man was talking about.

He answered her unspoken question. "Gifts, I think."

The fierce-looking woman laughed. "Is that what you call it?" She snorted. "Doesn't seem like such a gift to some of us."

"Enough, Tamryn." The man looked stern. "You go tell the others we're on our way."

Tamryn gave the man a look, but she did what he said. When she'd disappeared down the tunnel, the man turned back to the group and spoke to Pathik. "Your girl's fine."

Pathik, who had never spoken aloud of his feelings for Rachel, at least not to anyone but her, and *barely* even to her, found himself blushing. He gritted his teeth and held the man's gaze.

"Take us to her, then."

The man pointed to the others who had come from the north tunnel with Tamryn. They were already turning, heading back the way they had come. "Follow them," he said. "We'll be right behind you."

Pathik did so, with no hesitation. Malgam and Daniel conferred with their eyes for a moment, but they, Vivian and Nandy weren't far behind Pathik. The three men from the west tunnel brought up the rear.

Pathik wished they would move faster. He wanted to run, run ahead of these strangers who were leading him to Rachel, run as fast as he could to her side and see her safe and alive.

He hoped that these strangers really *were* leading him to Rachel.

Chapter 6

"I thought they decided to kill it." Tom didn't sound at all concerned about the screaming.

"Maybe that's what they're doing." Hannah shrugged, equally indifferent.

Rachel listened to their comments with growing horror, because she *knew* that scream. She'd only heard it once before, Away, on the night one of the Roberts had almost killed her, but she knew it.

The scream sounded again, even louder. This time it didn't stop.

"Where is he?" She couldn't see where the cries were coming from, but she ran toward the sound.

"That's Nipper!"

Rachel ignored Hannah and Tom, who ran after her. She hurried through groups of people, shocked faces staring at her as she went. She heard Tom reassuring those she passed, heard Hannah entreating her to stop. The cave was so large she couldn't see from one end to the other. Finally, she glimpsed another alcove of sorts along one wall. A crowd had gathered in front of the opening—the screams were coming from inside. Rachel pushed her way through the people to the front of the crowd.

There was a cage in the alcove, a metal cage that reminded Rachel of the one her father had been imprisoned in by the Roberts. Inside, pacing back and forth, lashing his tail and baring his fangs, was the Woolly she and the others had feared was dead.

"You're alive!" Rachel fell to the ground, holding on to the cage bars. "Nipper. We thought you were dead—all the blood back at the trail."

Nipper stopped screaming. He lifted his head, sniffed, opened his mouth halfway and sniffed again, his head bobbing ever so slightly.

"I'd get your hands away from the cage." A man stepped up to Rachel, extended his hand in an offer to help her stand.

Rachel stood without accepting the man's assistance. She saw the loop of rope at his side, the pointed stick he held. "Why do you have those? What are you doing to him?"

"We wanted to see if he'd be useful for

hunting, but he's too wild. He's going to hurt someone, so we're—"

"You're going to kill him." Rachel repeated the words Tom had said earlier.

"He's vicious." The man poked his stick through the bars at Nipper, who slashed at it with his claws. "We can't just let him roam the island." The man studied Nipper. "Never seen one like him here before."

"He's not vicious. He came with us." Rachel put her fingers inside the cage and whispered to the Woolly. "Nipper, it's me, Rachel. Nandy is alive, Nipper, she's fine. She'll be so happy to see you are, too."

Nipper flicked his ears forward at the sound of Nandy's name. He sniffed the air again and seemed to recognize Rachel's scent. When he moved toward the front of the cage she tensed a bit; she remembered how fierce Nipper was with almost everyone but Nandy. The man with the stick raised it, ready to stab it at the Woolly through the bars. But Nipper approached her slowly, and when he was close enough to her that she could feel the breath from his nostrils, he bowed his head and rubbed it against her fingers.

"It's going to be okay." Rachel ruffled the kinky fur on his head. The feline creature snuffled her hand and growled low in his throat. "I promise, Nipper."

"He was eating a sand mole when we came upon him." The man with the pointy stick, whose name turned out to be Ronald, sat at a table near the cage with Rachel and Hannah, his stick leaning on the bench next to him. Tom was standing next to the cage, watching Nipper groom himself. There was dried blood on his coat; Rachel had thought it was Nipper's at first. But according to Ronald all the blood belonged to a now-deceased sand mole. The blood Rachel and Pathik had found on the stone path had been from Nipper's prey, too. "I think that's the only reason we were able to get close. He was so hungry he didn't notice us until too late. We dozed him and brought him back here. Good thing we got him in the cage before he woke." There was a certain admiration in Ronald's tone.

"You people seem to do a lot of that." Rachel was worried. They wouldn't open the cage, no matter how much she insisted that Nipper wouldn't harm them. She didn't like him trapped like that—he'd have no chance against their pointed sticks if they decided he was too much of a risk.

"Look, at least they didn't kill him, and you know dozing doesn't harm you . . ." Hannah looked a bit embarrassed; she must have been remembering that Rachel knew from personal experience.

"He's so big!" Tom didn't take his eyes off Nipper. "He's all muscle, too."

"Let him go." Rachel turned to Ronald. "Just let him go and you can keep me here for as long as you want." Rachel didn't mean a word of it.

"We can *already* do that." Sarah strode up to the table. "I thought you were taking care of that." She nodded at the Woolly and gave Ronald a look. He shrugged, abashedly.

"He started making a fuss the minute we got near the cage. I was waiting on a dozer—so he wouldn't suffer—but nobody was available. I decided to go ahead and just get it over with because he was so wild." Ronald ran a hand over his beard nervously. "But this one ran over and—"

"So I hear." Sarah didn't look pleased. "Well, we've got other things to tend to right now." She took hold of Rachel's arm, hauling her up from the table. "You'll be coming with me."

"I'm not going anywhere until you let Nipper out of that cage." Rachel wrenched her arm free from Sarah's grip.

"You don't have much choice." Sarah grabbed Rachel's arm again, her voice low and hard.

"Sarah." A woman glided up to the group, smiling. She was slight, with gray hair down to her waist. Her expression was serene but there was something in her eyes; embers awaiting tinder, ready to flame. "We need to escort our visitor to her people, but not in that manner, surely." The woman turned to Rachel, her gaze oddly intent. "I haven't heard what your name is yet, friend."

Rachel realized it was true. Not a single person had asked her what her name was, not even Hannah. "My name is Rachel." The rest of the woman's words sunk in then. "Are my friends here?"

"I am Filina." The woman held out her hand. Her gaze sharpened even more.

Rachel didn't take the woman's hand. "Are my friends here or not?"

Filina smiled again, though it seemed strained. "They are. I sent Sarah to fetch you but you seem reluctant to leave this creature alone."

"This *creature* is named Nipper, and your people were about to kill him." Rachel wanted nothing more than to go to wherever Pathik and the others were, but she didn't trust this woman. "Bring them here, to me." She waited, but Filina didn't respond to her demand. "Bring my friends *here*."

Filina stared at Rachel's face, but she didn't seem to be seeing it. After a moment she turned to Sarah. "We'll join you in the office shortly."

Sarah looked from Filina to Rachel and back again. She seemed surprised about something, though Rachel was so angry about Nipper that she barely noticed. Filina raised an eyebrow. "Sarah, I *said* we'll be along shortly. Now go."

Sarah stalked off, but she looked back twice, a speculative expression on her face.

Filina returned her gaze to Rachel. She stared at her for another long moment. "I give you my word nothing will be done to . . . Nipper, while you're gone. Now, let's go, shall we?" She extended her hand again, keeping her eyes on Rachel's.

This time, Rachel took Filina's hand. She felt like there was some sort of fog in her mind, a gray fuzziness that impeded her thoughts. She followed meekly behind Filina without a single glance back at Nipper.

"Rachel!" Vivian rushed forward and wrapped her arms around the girl, burying her face in

Rachel's hair.

"Mom." Rachel felt strange, as though she had just snapped back to reality from a hazy dream. She looked around the room Filina had led her to—it was wooden structure built against one wall of the larger cavern. There was a door set into a wooden frame, closed now so that none of the noise in the main cave was audible in the room. In the center of the room was a long table, with chairs on either side. Daniel, Malgam and Nandy stood near the table, and Pathik, too. There were three others in the room; Jim, the man who had dozed Pathik and her, was seated at the table. David, the other man who had been in the group that took her, sat next to him. Across from them sat Sarah, a sour look on her face.

Pathik waited while Daniel held his daughter, waited while Vivian hugged her again, while Malgam and Nandy greeted her. He stood back, watching, searching her face. Finally, when everyone else had had their turn, he approached. "Did they hurt you?" Pathik looked straight into Rachel's eyes.

"I'm fine." Rachel felt her cheeks flush. She wanted to touch Pathik. She wanted to feel that he was real. "I was worried about *you*."

Pathik smiled then, just a slight upturn of his lips. He stepped close, put his arms around her and held her. Rachel let herself relax into his arms.

"We're having a meal brought in—I'm sure you all must be hungry." Filina gestured to the table. "Now that you can see your girl is unharmed, shall we sit? We have a lot to talk about." Everyone began to take their places at the long table.

"They have Nipper!" Rachel blurted it out. It felt like something she'd just remembered. As soon as she said the words, she felt the strange, foggy feeling in her mind again. She shook her head, fighting to clear it away.

Nandy froze, half-seated. "Where?"

Filina stared at Nandy. "Nipper is fine. We can see to him after we talk."

Nandy sat down.

Rachel couldn't believe it. *Nandy sat down.* After hearing that Nipper, her beloved Woolly, was here, she just sat down.

Something here was very wrong. Rachel frowned. "But don't you want—" The fogginess reappeared, and for a moment she couldn't remember what she had been about to say.

There was a knock on the door.

"Ah, here they are." Filina sounded pleased. "Some lunch for our guests."

A young woman entered, followed by two boys, all laden with trays of food. They placed the trays on the table along with dishes and a pitcher of water, then left as silently as they'd come. Filina poured water for everyone. "Come now, eat. After what I'm told you've been through you must welcome the sight of a hearty meal."

The food did look good. There was bread and a soft cheese, along with a plump, round fruit Rachel had never seen before, but she was still full from the stew Tom had brought her. She sat next to Pathik and watched the others fill their plates. They all ate with gusto, silent until their stomachs were full. Rachel noticed Sarah watching her a few times, but she always looked away when Rachel met her gaze.

"Now then." Filina sat back in her chair. "We need to apologize, first, for the way we introduced ourselves to you." She laughed lightly, as though abducting Rachel was a simple matter of a misunderstanding. "But you have to understand, we can't take chances. We've sacrificed much to make this island a safe place and we had no idea who you were." She looked around the table at Rachel and the others.

"We were told . . ." Daniel hesitated. "That is, we were under the impression that this might be a safe place for us, too. It appears we may have been wrong about that."

"You weren't wrong. It's just . . . there have been people in the past, people who aren't like us. They didn't mean us any good." Filina looked troubled. "We just had to be certain you weren't like them."

"Do you mean Regs?" Malgam crossed his arms. "Well, I mean, some of us here are Regs." He looked at Vivian and Daniel, then at Rachel.

"Regs." Filina tried the term out. "Is that what you call those with no talent?"

Malgam shook his head. "That's what we call the ones who stayed safe from the bombs, the ones on the U.S. side of things. At least, the ones we still don't like." He smiled at Rachel. "By talent I assume you mean our gifts. Plenty of us where I'm from have no gift."

"Really?" David spoke for the first time. "None at all? We *all* have something, here. I thought maybe these four didn't because they weren't from the bombed areas."

Malgam studied David. "Which four?" He got no answer. "How do you know how many of us have a gift and how many don't?" He leaned forward across the table.

There was silence around the table. David exchanged a look with Filina, who gave him a slight nod.

"That's *my* talent." David spoke the words like a challenge. "I can tell whether a person has anything and I can tell how much. You, for instance," he narrowed his eyes at Malgam, "have some talent, but it's not very strong. In fact, neither you nor the boy are very heavy hitters." He smirked then, as though he'd dealt Malgam some sort of satisfying blow. "The rest of you—" David looked curiously at Nandy. "I don't get anything solid from the rest."

"They don't have amps though, and probably never had honers work with them either. You said yourself the whole colony seemed crude at best, in terms of talent." Sarah's eyes widened when she realized Filina was looking at her, a displeased expression on her face.

"What's a honer?" Pathik was about to ask more, but Daniel interrupted him.

"Colony? Do you mean our people Away?" Daniel frowned at Filina. "How long have you known about us? Why didn't you make any attempt to contact us?"

Filina raised an eyebrow. "I think we all have a lot to talk about." She turned to Pathik. "A honer is someone who can help you get better at your tal—at your *gift*, Pathik. We can probably assign you one, help you improve, once we've got you all settled in here." She turned back to Daniel. "That is, if you plan to stay here with us? I'm assuming you do, since you came all this way."

Nandy spoke, as if she'd just roused herself from a trance. "I want to see Nipper."

Chapter 7

When Nandy saw the cage, she went straight for the lock. Before she could hack at it more than once with her knife, Ronald ran over and waved a rusty key at her.

"I'll unlock it! That's one of our last locks, woman! Stop cutting at it."

Nandy stopped mid-swing and stepped back. "Get to it then."

"Wait." Filina held up a hand. "How do we know this thing—Nipper—won't tear someone apart? We have children here."

Nandy knelt next to the cage and called to

Nipper. The Woolly came directly to her, purring loudly. He nuzzled her hand through the cage bars. "He's not going to hurt anyone."

Filina looked doubtful, but she gave Ronald a signal to go ahead. He approached the cage door with key in hand, trying not to look nervous. Nipper growled, as though he was an exonerated king admonishing an errant jailer. Ronald fumbled with the lock and finally clicked it open. He did not open the door to the cage. Instead, he stepped back, picked up his pointed stick and nodded to Nandy.

The minute the cage door opened, Nipper leapt out and wrapped his front legs around Nandy's neck. She almost toppled from his enthusiasm. Ronald, misunderstanding the display, raised his stick, and immediately Nipper was facing him, claws out and roaring. Nandy jumped up and put herself between Ronald and Nipper, doing her best to calm the Woolly.

Pathik joined Nandy in front of Nipper. "Put your spear down!"

"I thought he was attacking the woman." Ronald lowered his weapon very slowly.

"Like I said, he won't hurt anyone—as long as they don't try to hurt him. Or anyone he thinks of as his family." Nandy spoke the words loudly, so that the rest of the crowd that had gathered could hear them. She turned and stroked Nipper's head, making soothing noises.

One of the people in the crowd, a woman, stepped forward. "They'll be staying, then?" Rachel recognized her as the second woman of the group that had kidnapped her. She could see the woman in her mind, just as she had been at that moment on the path—her eyes closed, her face focused. Rachel thought the woman had had something to do with her not being able to make any noise when she tried to scream.

"They will." Filina pasted a smile on a millisecond too late. "They've come to live in peace, as we do."

"Will they be taking part in Celebration?" The woman didn't look happy.

"Not this one, surely, Liza. It's too soon. They need time to settle in."

Liza said nothing.

"Well then." Filina turned to look at the people who had gathered around the cage. "All of you have preparations to make, don't you? As Liza has reminded us, Celebration is in less than two days. I'd suggest we all get back to work." She took a deep breath, closed her eyes for a moment.

People began to wander away, back to whatever they had been doing, some in groups, some alone. There were some whispers, some backward glances, but for the most part they all did as Filina asked.

"Celebration?" Pathik asked the question all of them were thinking. "What's that?"

Filina just smiled. "Time enough for explanations later. All of you must be tired. We'll get you settled in quarters and let you rest." She crinkled her brow. "I'm afraid our largest available family quarters may be a bit small for your whole group."

"We could split into two—Rachel, Daniel and myself, and Malgam, Nandy and Pathik." Vivian looked at the others questioningly.

"If the rooms are close to each other." Malgam scowled.

"Of course." Filina noticed Hannah and Tom standing near. "Hannah. You can show them their rooms—the two empty units on the west wall. Tom, you can get bedding, whatever they might need."

Tom left at a trot. Hannah stepped closer to Rachel, but she kept her eyes on Nipper, as though he might leap on her at any moment.

"He really won't hurt you," Rachel whispered.

Hannah didn't look so certain. "He's so scary-looking."

"I know—I was scared the first time I met him, too."

"Hannah." Filina looked less than pleased. "Take them along now, and then get back to help Sarah with the preparations."

"We'd better go." Hannah waited until she was sure everyone in the group was together. "Just follow me—it's not too far." She practically skipped along, turning once to check that everyone was following. They wound through groups of people, all working. One woman watched several toddlers, each with a long length of twine tied onto their clothing, the ends held in her hands. Rachel wondered at that, though she could see how easy it might be to lose a child in the immense cavern. The woman seemed kind enough, patiently handing back a dropped toy, checking a scratched knee. She smiled at Rachel when the group passed her.

Two younger boys and an old man kneaded dough at a table. Several loaves of it were already shaped, rising in shallow wooden bowls. One of the boys stared at Pathik as they passed.

"What do you think Celebration is?" Pathik whispered, eyes on the boy.

Rachel shrugged. "I bet we're going to find out soon enough."

"I wonder if we want to know." Pathik stared back at the boy with the bread dough.

"Here we are." Hannah turned to the group. "Those are the units." She pointed toward two wooden doors set into the cave wall. They were two in a row of many, all identical. "They're pretty big inside. Keith made them, before he left—" Hannah stopped abruptly. "Well, anyway." She opened the first door. "Tom should be back soon with bedding and things."

Tom *was* back, almost as soon as Hannah spoke the words. He towed a dented child's wagon filled with blankets and oil lights and other supplies, and the packs containing all the group's belongings, which they'd left in the room Filina called the office. He and Hannah helped unload everything.

"I brought this," said Tom, holding up a bowl of chopped meat. "It's sand mole—I figured since he was hunting it he might like it." Tom looked at Nipper, who was watching him with suspicion.

"Thank you." Nandy took the bowl. "I bet he'll love it."

Tom and Hannah took their leave, and the

group began to settle in.

The units were fairly large, at least for rooms that had been carved out of rock. Each had a main room, a bedroom and a small bathroom. Daniel and Malgam checked the second unit out while Rachel, Pathik, Nandy and Vivian unpacked some of their things in the first.

"Looks like they work the bathrooms just like we did Away." Pathik held a curtain back from the bathroom doorway to reveal a chamber pot. "I guess The Property spoiled me a bit. I miss the hot and cold running water and the flushing toilet, even though I barely got to know them." He grinned at Rachel.

"Should we all stay in this one tonight?" Nandy looked around the main room of the first unit. "It would be tight, but it might be better if we're all together."

"We don't want to put them on the defensive right away." Daniel came through the door, Malgam right behind him. "The other one is exactly like this one. It's almost like they've got a little city in this cavern."

"This doesn't look like it was done by hand." Rachel pointed to the walls. The carving was smooth like the upper walls of the alcove had been, too smooth to have been done with crude hand tools.

"Keith." Vivian recalled the name Hannah had mentioned. "Who do you suppose Keith is—or was? That girl said he made these *before* . . . something." She ran a hand over one of the walls. "I wonder if this was his talent."

Malgam, ever practical, started splitting up the box of food Tom had brought, placing some in a separate pile to take to the unit next door. "I think Daniel is right about not putting our hosts on edge. We should be fine tonight with some of us in here and some of us in there. But for now, let's talk about what we want to do from here."

They borrowed a bench and a stool from the second unit so they could all sit around the small table in the first. Rachel felt safe for the first time since they had climbed into the boat and headed to the island. She was so relieved that her mother and father, Pathik and Malgam and Nandy, even Nipper, were all alive and with her. She felt Pathik's hand touch hers under the table.

"For tonight at least, I think we should take shifts keeping watch." Nandy kept her voice low, as though she thought someone might be listening. She petted Nipper, who leaned against her knee.

"I agree." Malgam eyed the closed door. "But in the meantime, I think we should do a little exploring. See what we can find out."

"I have a feeling Filina expects us to stay in the units, for now." Vivian sounded hesitant. "Do you think she'd want us wandering around?"

Malgam snorted. "I could not care less what she'd want us to—"

"I think we're all exhausted." Daniel rubbed his eyes. "We do need to find out what's going on here, but for tonight, let's regroup and rest. We may need our strength."

Rachel watched her father, saw how he sagged against the table as though he could barely stay upright. He'd been through so much when the Roberts took him, and he still wasn't fully recovered. Malgam was stronger, but he, too, was recovering from the illness that had almost killed him. They both needed rest desperately.

"Pathik and I can take a look around, then come back and take second watch." Rachel looked at Vivian. "Maybe you and Nandy could take first watch?"

Vivian understood immediately. "That's a perfect idea. Nandy?"

Nandy nodded. She and Vivian exchanged a look—they were both worried about the men. Nandy put a hand on Pathik's shoulder. "As long as you two don't wander far." She stood. "Let's get the beds made up."

With everyone working it took no time at all to ready the beds in both units. There were two in each—a bed and a sort of cot. Rachel knew she and Pathik would be sleeping in the cots, but they looked fairly comfortable. The bedding was finer than anything Away—it seemed closer to the sort of thing Rachel and Vivian had been used to on the Unified States side of the Line.

"Where do you suppose they get these?" Vivian stroked a soft, fine blanket. "Any from before the bombs would have rotted long ago." She handed the blanket to Nandy, who was ready to finish up the last bed. "There was nothing this fine Away, was there?" Vivian had only spent a short time Away before they'd left for the island.

Nandy shook her head. "We had a couple of looms we used, but you can see what they turned out." She fingered the sleeve of her own shirt. "Rough stuff, compared to this."

"Stone that looks shaped by machines, fine sheets." Malgam frowned. "I didn't see any evidence of a power source. I know Indigo thought they might still have power from the wind farm that was supposed to have been here, but they're using oil lamps for light and buckets for toilets. If the wind farm was still operational they'd at least have lights."

Pathik caught Rachel's eye. "We'll go wander a bit," he said to Nandy. "See what we can see."

"Remember, not too far." Nandy gave the blanket a shake and let it fall onto the bed.

"Don't forget your jacket." Vivian handed Rachel her coat.

Rachel smiled and shrugged it on. She put her hands in the pockets and felt the orchid cubes she had stashed there during the storm. When she pulled them out, Vivian gasped.

"Oh, Rachel! Your orchids." Vivian's eyes were brimming with tears.

"Mom, what's wrong?" Rachel went to her mother, who took the cubes like they were expensive crystal goblets.

"I didn't want to tell you, but . . ." Vivian dabbed at her eyes. "The rest—the ones you and Elizabeth packed—they all got ruined by saltwater. I thought they were all dead."

Rachel felt her own tears threatening to fall.

She had feared that the flat of orchid cubes was lost—it was the reason she'd taken these two and stuffed them in her coat during the storm—but she'd hoped that she was wrong. She thought about how she'd worked with Ms. Moore in the greenhouse just before they left for Away, carefully packing the orchid crosses one by one in the cubes, preserving them in the hope they might thrive in a new world. Ms. Moore knew then that she wasn't going to Cross with the rest of them, that she would stay with Jonathan on The Property, waiting, hoping for a miracle: that Indigo was still alive. Both she and Rachel had known that day that if he was still alive, he wouldn't be for long.

"Two is enough." Rachel tried to keep her voice from shaking. She checked the fluid levels in the two cubes her mother held. Still plenty of nutrient solution in both. "Two will be enough for me to propagate more." She watched as Vivian placed them on the table. The tiny green plants inside the cubes glowed with life.

Rachel took it as a good sign. Maybe things here would be what Indigo had thought they could be. Maybe they could start again, find a way to make a life together. She let her gaze linger on the cubes a moment more. She'd have to find them light—they couldn't live long in the cave.

"Let's go." Pathik waited at the door.

Rachel gave Vivian a hug and turned to join him. They stepped through the unit door and stood outside a moment, scanning the cavern.

"Where to?" Rachel was glad the units weren't

in the middle of the cave. There were enough eyes on them as it was—she felt like shrinking before the stares from people nearby.

"We were hoping you might get to come out for a while!" Hannah appeared from nowhere, Tom right behind her, both of them beaming. "We can show you around some more, if you'd like."

Pathik glanced at Rachel, then withdrew his hand from his knife as surreptitiously as he could. "That would be . . . nice." He didn't sound like he thought it would be nice at all.

Chapter 8

All the living spaces are along the perimeter of the cave. You're in one of the newer sections, where they're all rock. Over there," Hannah pointed across the vast space of the cavern, "are the older ones, from the beginning."

Rachel and Pathik could see wood-framed structures like the room they called the office, built lean-to style along the perimeter of the far wall.

"The beginning?" Rachel stayed close to Pathik as they followed Hannah and Tom on the tour.

"Way back, when the bombs fell." Tom shrugged. "They didn't have talent, those first survivors, so they couldn't make them the way the new ones are made. Although with Keith gone, we may have to go back to—" He didn't finish. "Most of the people left out here died from the radiation in the beginning. Was it the same for you?"

Pathik nodded. "Most of the people Away died, too. For a long time, no babies survived. When they did, they usually had a gift. Now, most of us do."

"*Most* of you." Tom frowned. "I think at first we only had some people with talent, but now it's everyone. Everyone has something, even if it's just pinging." He gave Hannah a sly glance, which she made a great show of ignoring. "I wonder what the difference is?"

"Don't know." Pathik was scanning everything they passed as they walked, trying to memorize all the details. He kept an eye out for exits, but didn't see any.

"Maybe honers?" Rachel had been wondering about the difference herself. "Like Sarah said in the office. I don't think there were any honers Away, were there Pathik?"

Pathik shook his head. "Nothing like here. We would practice on our focus in Usage, get better at our gifts that way, but it sounds like honers can do more than that."

"They can." Tom grinned. "Before I was honed I didn't really understand what I was getting from people—with my talent, I mean. I knew I felt different around someone who was healthy than I did around someone who wasn't, but I couldn't tell what it was that made me feel that way. I didn't know how to read what I was feeling. A honer can narrow it down for you, teach you how to work with what you've got."

"Maybe that's the difference. Since you have honers here, maybe they just helped everyone develop their gifts better." Rachel stopped walking. "Maybe everyone Away has a gift, too, but without someone to bring it out—like a honer—they don't all know it."

"Makes sense, in a way. We all come from people who got exposed to the bombs, and that's what causes the gifts, isn't it?" Pathik started walking again. "Is the cave entrance we came in the only one?"

Hannah and Tom exchanged another look. Neither replied. After a moment, Tom pointed toward the benches that had made Rachel think of the council room Away. "That's where we hold meetings, to decide things like who's doing what jobs, or how—"

"Look." Pathik cut Tom off. "Are we actually guests here, or prisoners?" He asked the question quietly, but Rachel could hear the challenge in his voice.

Tom heard it, too. He stopped walking and waited until Pathik stopped, too. "As far as Hannah and I are concerned, you're guests." Tom looked around him to see if anyone was watching them. "I thought the idea was that you wanted to start new here—is that right?"

"As far as *you* two are concerned." Rachel

ignored Tom's question and asked one of her own. "What about the rest of the people here?"

Once again, Hannah and Tom were silent. Finally, Hannah stepped closer to Rachel and whispered.

"Most of the people here are just like us." She looked around like Tom had, checking to see if they could be overheard. "They don't want any trouble. As long as you don't plan on causing any, they'll welcome you all here."

"What sort of trouble would we be planning on causing?" Rachel watched Hannah and Tom.

Hannah shrugged. "I guess there was a lot of fighting here at first about how to run things, but that was back when the bombs first hit, and everyone was panicked about surviving. They figured out a system—they elect council members and have lots of meetings before they decide on things—it works pretty well. It's been that way forever. A few years back we had some trouble from outside for a while. But we've had peace here for a long time now."

"At a cost." Tom made the comment in such a way that it was obvious he and Hannah had had many discussions about the subject.

"From outside?" Rachel wondered what that meant. Outside the cave? Outside the island?

"Hannah. Tom." A woman called from some distance. She approached them, threading her way through groups of people. When she got closer she noticed Rachel and Pathik, and slowed. After a moment she resumed her pace and when she reached them she put her hands on her hips. "Didn't I say not to be late for dinner?"

Hannah grinned. "Ma, we have our own unit now. We can get our own dinner if we don't eat at general."

"Your food's always better than what they serve at general, though." Tom gave the woman a charming look.

"Are these the new ones?" The woman ignored Tom and eyed Rachel and Pathik.

"Two of them." Hannah shot an apologetic look at Rachel. "Sorry, Ma's not in a polite mood right now, I guess." She grinned again when her mother grimaced. "Ma," she said, making a formal gesture toward Rachel, "this is Rachel. And this," she indicated Pathik, "is her . . . are you two formally attached yet?"

Pathik blushed deep red. Rachel looked at the ground, unsure what to do. They'd never talked about what was between them—not in that way, anyway. The future seemed so uncertain most of the time that Rachel didn't let herself think about what it might mean to say more than *I love you*, and she suspected it was even more complex for Pathik. He was one of the Others, she was a Reg. Even Pathik's grandfather, Indigo, hadn't been able to make that kind of love work, and Rachel wondered sometimes if Pathik thought of that, too.

"Have to get a unit of your own soon if you are, won't you?' Hannah's mother barreled right over the discomfort Pathik and Rachel were feeling. "Rachel, good to meet you. And your name, son?"

"Pathik."

Hannah's mother nodded, then smirked at Hannah. "Looks like I can still teach you a thing or two about manners."

"What about that dinner?" Tom looked behind him at the number of eyes fixed on them. "We could stand to get out of the general glare right now, anyway."

"Well then, off we go. And you two come eat with us tonight. There's plenty to go around." Hannah's mother started off without looking to see if anyone followed.

"We should let our parents know." Rachel looked to Pathik, who nodded his agreement.

"Polly can do that. Let's go." Hannah beckoned for them to follow her and set off after her mother.

"Her little sister," explained Tom. "She'll run a note over to them once we get there."

The unit they entered was similar to the ones they had been assigned, but it felt like a home. The main room was filled with the trappings of family life—neatly folded clothes in a pile on one of the chairs, a tattered cloth doll abandoned in a corner, a table set for dinner, and wonderful smells wafting up out of various serving dishes.

"Have a seat there," said Hannah's mother, pointing at the table. "Polly! Polly, come out here."

From one of three doorways off the main room, a child of about ten poked her head. Her eyes rounded when she saw Rachel and Pathik and she practically leapt into the room. "You're the strangers!" The child stared, her expression so awe-struck that Rachel had to laugh.

"I'm Rachel, and this is Pathik." Rachel smiled at the girl. "Are you Polly?'

"I am." Polly turned suddenly shy, hiding behind her mother's legs.

"Now, child. We need you to run a message over to the new folks in those units at the end of Sarah's row." Hannah's mother shuffled through the contents of a box that she took from a shelf mounted on the stone wall, and retrieved a scrap of paper and a sharpened stub of charcoal. "This will do." She handed the items to Rachel. "You can write a note and Polly will run it over."

The back of the scrap of paper had some sort of advertisement printed on it. Rachel tried to read it but most of it was so faded that it was illegible. She held the pointed charcoal over the paper. "Where shall I say we are?"

Hannah's mother looked confused for a moment. "Oh. Yes. I'm Annie. Say you're at Annie and Leon's—anyone will know how to direct them if need be."

"Pleased to meet you, Annie." Rachel scribbled a note and handed it to Polly, who took it with an air of gravity. "My mother's name is Vivian. She'll be glad to meet you, Polly."

"Be quick, Polly. Dinner's ready." Annie watched Polly skip out the door. She shook her head. "That child cannot *walk* anywhere." She took three small pieces of wood from a stack on the floor in a corner. On the far wall of the unit there was a blackened metal, box-like contraption. Annie carried the wood to it, opened the front of it like it was a cupboard and tucked the wood inside.

"A stove!" Pathik stood to get a closer look. "How do you handle the smoke?"

Annie looked proud. "This unit is one of the first Keith did. Got a stove and an extra bedroom, too." She frowned. "They reduced the sizes a while back, but we got this one before that. Smoke goes right up a tube he made, through to the outside, with baffles to diffuse it so nobody sees it who shouldn't." She removed the lid of a tin pot on the top of the stove and stirred the contents with a wooden spoon. "Council wanted to prohibit us using these last session, said the smoke was too much of a risk even baffled. Said we should stick with the community ovens where the cooking is all done at night. But those who have these little stoves are of the oldest stock—they were made by the first survivors. We carry some weight. And it's nice to be able to make your own family a dinner, when you want."

"Now if you'd just use that weight in ways that would make a difference." Tom grumbled the words, not looking at Annie.

"Enough of that for now, Thomas." Annie carried the tin pot to the table. "Our guests don't need to know all about our disagreements."

"Who is this Keith?" asked Rachel. "And where did he go?"

Everyone was silent. Annie shifted uncomfortably, Tom looked angry, and Hannah looked worried.

"Now, who told you he went anywhere?" Annie spooned stew from the pot into the dishes on the table.

Rachel looked at Hannah. She wondered if she'd be getting her in trouble if she revealed that Hannah had been the one to say Keith was gone.

"I did." Hannah shrugged. "I was telling them about their units and it just slipped out. They'll know soon enough anyway."

"Look who I found flitting around outside." A man entered the unit, Polly right behind him. He was one of the tallest men Rachel had ever seen, and there was a jolliness in his expression that made her feel instantly comfortable. "Dinner ready?"

"We've got guests tonight." Annie went to the man and gave him a hug. "Where've you been?"

"A meeting." The man looked at Pathik and Rachel. "I'm pleased to welcome you both. I'm Leon, Hannah's father. And father to this little sprite, as well." He made a playful swipe in Polly's direction. She shrieked and ran around the table.

"Pleased to meet you, Sir." Pathik stood.

"Sit, sit." Leon smiled and sat himself, easing his length onto the bench at the head of the table. "Polly says your note was delivered."

Polly nodded. "Your Ma is nice," she said, looking at Rachel. "She gave me a sweet."

Rachel thought of the meager supplies they had saved from the wreckage of their boat. Vivian must have found some sort of treat in the emergency food rations. "She is nice, isn't she? Was she okay with us staying here for dinner?"

Polly nodded. "She said, don't be too long. They *always* do say that." Polly rolled her eyes at Annie.

"Well, time to eat, then, so we don't make these two late." Annie passed slices of seed-filled bread to each of the diners. For a time all talk ceased as trays and bowls were passed. When everyone had dinner on their plates, Leon looked around the table and uttered a sort of prayer.

"Keep our family—and our new friends—safe. That's all we can ask for. Let's eat."

And eat they did. The food was plain, with few spices, but they had salt in abundance and that helped. Rachel watched Pathik make quick work of his stew and felt grateful, once again, that he was alive.

"You two and the rest of your group are the subject of speculation tonight." Leon slurped the last of his stew from his bowl.

"Hannah said you don't get many visitors here." Rachel smiled at Hannah, remembering how she'd suggested that this might be due to the welcome visitors seemed to receive. Hannah grinned back.

"Not many, that's for certain." Leon dabbed daintily at his lips with a cloth napkin. Then he belched.

"Leon!" Annie flapped her napkin at him. "Can you *not,* please?"

Leon just grinned. "Good food deserves a good burp, my love." He turned his attention back to Rachel and Pathik. "So you come from that colony on the mainland, then?"

Pathik nodded. "We call it Away. How long have you known about it?"

Leon arched a brow. "I think they knew long ago. As long as I can remember, anyway. Just stories, for the most part, about another place that got left out on the wrong side of the border systems, a place that got blown to bits like us. Just stories, until David was born, that is. When he got older we realized his talent. He definitely felt, well, *talent*, from that direction. So we knew there were people. Just didn't know what kind of people you might turn out to be."

"You don't *seem* like savages." Polly eyed Rachel and Pathik brightly.

"Polly!" Hannah shushed her little sister.

"Savages." Pathik said the word softly. "Is that what you call us?"

Annie stood and began gathering the plates. "Apologies, young man." She frowned at Polly. "There's rumors about the colony, that's all. Always have been—just talk from people who don't know what's over there." She set the plates on a work table that stood against the wall. "You'll be cleaning those tonight, miss," she said to Polly.

"We didn't know about you, either." Pathik still spoke quietly, but there was something in his voice that made Rachel nervous. "We only hoped you existed. But I never heard any stories about how you were savages."

"Don't mind the stories, son." Leon waited

until Pathik looked up. "Most here will judge you for what you are, not what they've heard. People tell all sorts of tales when they're scared, scared of everything. We've all been scared of everything for generations, here." He titled his head. "Is it the same there—Away? You folks were left just like us, left to die. I imagine you have some stories about that, coming up through the years."

Pathik thought about it. "I guess so. And I guess there are savages, Away." He looked at Rachel. "The Roberts."

Rachel nodded. "But they weren't your people." She turned to the others at the table. "Pathik's people are good. The Roberts were a neighboring clan."

"And are the Roberts why you all wanted to get away from . . . Away?" Tom spoke for the first time since they'd started eating. "Were they causing enough trouble that you had to leave? Or did you have to leave for some other reason?"

"You want to know if we were forced to go." Pathik met Tom's gaze. "We weren't. We didn't do anything wrong, if that's what you're worried about."

"Not worried, so much. Just wanted to check." Tom didn't look away from Pathik. "We don't want any more trouble here than we already have."

Pathik nodded. "That's what I'd really like to talk about." He took a sip of water from the chipped glass in front of him. "What kind of trouble do you already have, Tom?"

Chapter 9

Do you think we should go get them?" Vivian was sitting at the table, fretting.

"They'll be fine." Daniel didn't look as certain as he sounded.

Malgam finished splitting up the supplies. "We'll give them a little more time—eating dinner with those people might give them a chance to find some things out. But not too long." He picked up one of the boxes of supplies. "I'll take this to the other unit."

Nandy watched him go with worried eyes. She stroked Nipper absently, glad to hear the low rumble of his purr. The fact that he seemed comfortable here reassured her; she didn't think he would have relaxed if there was imminent danger. Nipper looked up at her as though he knew she was thinking about him and blinked slowly, once. "I think Pathik and Rachel can take care of themselves. They've learned a lot about that, recently."

"I just wish we knew what to expect from these people." Vivian massaged her temples, fatigue finally hitting her.

Malgam returned from the other unit, but before he could sit down again a knock sounded on the door. Everyone looked at each other, unspoken questions hanging in the air between them. Malgam retraced his steps and opened the door. When he stepped aside, Sarah entered the unit.

"I just came by to see that you're all settled." She hovered near the door.

Daniel stood. "Have a seat, won't you?" He gestured to an empty stool. "We were just waiting for Rachel and Pathik to come back."

"Come back?" Sarah looked uneasy. "I thought Filina wanted you to stay—"

"We're free to go where we please, aren't we?" Malgam had already seated himself. He glared at Sarah, who returned the look in kind.

"I'm not the one who decides what you're free to do." She turned to go.

"Wait, Sarah." Nandy stood and held out her hand. Nipper rose with her, all his attention on Sarah. "We don't mean to be rude." She shook her head when Malgam started to protest; that small gesture from her was all it took to silence him. "We just want to understand."

Sarah turned back. She sat on the stool that was offered, keeping her distance from Nipper. She looked around the room. "Have you got everything you need for the night?"

"We do." Nandy didn't add any thanks. She sat, too. Nipper gazed up at her and after she smiled, he resumed his place, leaning against her leg. "No one told us we couldn't leave the units."

Sarah looked behind her at the door. When she was satisfied that it was shut, she spoke, very quietly. "Where are Rachel and Pathik?"

"They went to have dinner with—"

"How does that matter?" Malgam interrupted Nandy. "Look, we came here in peace. If we're not welcome, we can—"

"It's not that you're not welcome." Sarah frowned. "I'm just trying to make sure they're with good people."

"They're with that girl, Hannah. And her friend." Vivian dismissed Malgam's look with a flick of her hand. "I want to know they're safe, Malgam."

Sarah looked relieved. "Hannah's family is fine. They'll be safe with them."

"It sounds like there are people they wouldn't be so safe with, though." Daniel leaned forward. "Is that right?"

Sarah looked at the door again. Then, she studied each of them in turn. "It's changing, here. There are . . . things happening, in the last few years, that don't seem right." She shook her head.

"Forgive me, but I'm taking a risk saying even that, and I don't know you people at all."

Daniel sat back, watching Sarah. Finally, he nodded, as if to himself. "We don't know you, either, Sarah. All we can do is try to show you we mean no harm. But it would help if we knew what we were getting into here. Who are the people we should be watching out for?"

Sarah sighed. "I don't think I can answer that." She shook her head, frustrated. "I don't think I know who they are, not really."

"I don't understand." Daniel kept watching Sarah's face.

"I don't know how to explain it." Sarah shrugged. "You'll see what I mean. At least maybe you will—in time." She turned her hands palm up on the table. "I know that sounds strange, but I haven't got more answers right now." She watched Nandy ruffle Nipper's fur. "You have quite a way with that animal."

"His name is Nipper," Nandy replied. "I helped him when he needed it—he was a baby—and I think it earned me his trust."

Sarah narrowed her eyes. "I think it might be more than that."

"What do you mean?" Nandy looked quizzical.

The door opened, startling everyone. Rachel and Pathik spilled in, laughing together about something. When they saw Sarah, they both stopped.

"Is everything all right?" Pathik looked across the table at Malgam, who nodded.

"See? Back safe and sound." Sarah rose from her stool. "I'll be going." She caught Nandy's eye. "Maybe tomorrow we can talk a bit." Then, she bid the group goodnight and left.

"They said we'll be formally introduced to the community tomorrow at the assembly." Rachel rubbed her eyes sleepily. "They're going to announce the Honoree of Celebration, too."

"What is this Celebration thing all about?" Malgam sounded skeptical.

"From the sounds of it, it's a way to mark another year of survival," said Pathik. "Hannah and Tom wouldn't tell us much else." He frowned. "They have all sorts of food, and there are games and they reveal this Honoree. Hannah's family was excited because they think she might be the Honoree this year. I think there's something strange about it."

"What's so strange about that?" Nandy raised an eyebrow.

"I think Pathik's right. There's something strange," said Rachel. "Hannah's parents were excited, but she wasn't, and neither was Tom. They both just looked . . . nervous."

"Nervous about Celebration?" Daniel waited while Rachel thought about it.

"I don't know. Hannah said Celebration is usually fun, and that there's a lot of good food and nobody has to work for the day. But I think she was nervous about the possibility that she would be chosen as Honoree. I think she was actually sort of frightened about it."

"Do you think she might just be shy, that the idea of being the center of attention might make her feel uneasy?" Vivian seemed hopeful that it could be explained that way.

Pathik and Rachel exchanged looks. "Maybe." Rachel was too tired to say much more. "Is it okay if I crawl into that cot and go to sleep? At least until my turn to take watch?"

"I think you'd all better get some rest. Vivian and I will stay up for first watch, right?"

Vivian nodded, and Nandy rose. "I'll leave our door open a crack, and you leave this one open, too, Vivian. That way if either of us needs help we can make enough noise that the other will hear."

Everyone hugged their goodnights, Pathik and Rachel still a bit awkward about showing any sort of affection in front of their parents. Nandy, Malgam and Pathik trooped out the door to the other unit.

Vivian added a blanket to the bedding already on the cot. "You get some rest Rachel, and you too, Daniel." She smiled at her husband. Then she sat back down at the table and stared at the tiny orchid starts. She listened to the sounds of her family as their breathing changed from waking rhythms to those of slumber. She listened hard for any sounds beyond their door, alert to all, ready to attack any threat with the particular fury a mother, a wife, a woman who loves, will bring.

Much later that night, Rachel sat at the same table, on the same stool, turning first one and then the other of the orchid cubes in her hands, inspecting the plants inside for signs of distress. Vivian was asleep, her turn at watch done, and Rachel was thinking of Pathik, who was in the next unit taking the same watch shift as her. She wondered what he was thinking about.

A sound from beyond the door brought her out of her reverie. She leaned her ear toward the door, waiting. Another rustle. Rachel crept toward the door and tried to see out of the tiny slit where it was open. She still couldn't see, but she could definitely hear something, just beyond her range of vision. She risked nudging the door open a bit more. A flash of movement, then a voice, whispering right into the crack.

"Can you come out?"

Rachel was so startled she stumbled backward a couple of steps. It was Hannah. She checked the bed: her parents were still sleeping. Slowly, she edged the door open enough to slip outside.

It was dark, the cave lit by only a few of the oil lights used during waking hours. Shadows of the flames flickered on the stone walls. Rachel couldn't see anyone stirring, though she assumed there must be guards posted at night. Hannah was crouched against the wall, as low as she could get.

"What are you doing out here?" Rachel crouched next to Hannah.

"I wanted to give you something." Hannah scanned the cavern. "I figured you might understand, because of Pathik. And you're the only person I can really trust right now. At least for this."

"What do you mean, because of Pathik?" Rachel could see from Hannah's face that whatever she had to say, it was serious.

"Because you love him." Hannah looked worried. "You do, don't you? Like I love Tom."

Rachel looked down the row of units to the one next to theirs, where she knew Pathik was awake behind the slightly opened door. "I do love him," she whispered, even more quietly than she had been already.

"Then you'll understand." Hannah held out a small packet. "I need you to keep this for me. Keep it hidden, and if I get chosen as Honoree, I need you to give it to Tom."

"What is it?" Rachel took the packet. It was made of fabric, sewn shut. It felt like there was paper inside.

"It's . . . it's me I guess. Me and Tom." Hannah bowed her head to hide them, but Rachel had seen the glint of tears. "It's all my thoughts and feelings about us, things that only he and I know. Things that make me—make me myself." She wiped her cheek with the back of her hand, and smiled. "It may be they'll choose someone else, and then it won't be important, but if they don't, you've got to promise you'll give it to him."

"I don't understand." Rachel reached out toward Hannah. "What is all this about the Honoree? What happens—"

"Shouldn't you be home in bed, Hannah?" Filina's voice was silky, calm. She walked toward the two girls silently.

Rachel shoved the packet in her coat, wondering how Filina had managed to just appear, as if from nowhere. "We were just having some girl-talk. It's my fault. I asked Hannah if she could meet me."

"Hannah's got a big day tomorrow." Filina smiled at them. "We all have extra work preparing for Celebration."

Hannah got up. "Sorry, Filina, I didn't mean any harm. I'm on my way."

"I'll walk you home." Filina put an arm around Hannah's shoulders and they started walking away. "You should probably get some rest, too, Rachel," she said, not bothering to turn around.

Rachel felt a chill then, though the cave wasn't cold, really. She watched them until they had disappeared. She was turning to go back into the unit when she noticed the door of Pathik's was open wider than it had been before.

"Pathik?" She whispered the word.

He stepped out then, just enough so that she could see him. "Are you okay?"

"Were you there the whole time?"

He nodded. "I had to be sure you were okay."

"Did you hear what she said?"

He nodded again. "Something's wrong." He looked behind him, into the unit. When he turned back to her, he made a motion with his head, indicating that Malgam and Nandy were stirring. "We'll talk tomorrow."

It wasn't until Daniel had relieved her of watch and she was curled under the blankets on the cot that Rachel realized: Pathik must have heard her say she loved him. She smiled. But then, she frowned. Why was it so hard, just to say it? It felt like a risk to her, every time. Like she might lose him just because she told the world what he meant to her. She wondered if it was the same for him.

Chapter 10

There were so many people. Rachel thought there must be over a thousand. The crowd was relatively quiet for one of that size; people stood in loose groups talking softly. Some of the older people sat on benches or stools, their families gathered around them, everyone facing the raised platform in the center of the large assembly area. There was a feeling in the air, whether of anticipation or of dread, Rachel could not tell.

The cave was lit with so many lamps a false day seemed to have dawned. Smoke, black and sooty, drifted down, floating like oil on water. Some people had fans made of a bit of paper, or a scrap of thin metal, which they waved to disperse it. Rachel scanned the crowd for a glimpse of Hannah and found her, standing next to Tom. Not far behind them were Hannah's parents and her little sister, Polly. When Hannah saw Rachel, she waved, a small, much more tentative gesture than Rachel would have ever expected from her.

Rachel and Pathik had told the others about Hannah's late night visit. Over a hasty breakfast the group had tried to figure out what was going on.

"So, being chosen as Honoree is a compliment according to Hannah's mother, but Hannah and Tom don't seem to agree." Daniel squinted. "Did Hannah say what was involved?"

"No." Rachel shook her head. "She just said that if she was chosen I needed to give Tom the packet. Like she wouldn't be able to."

"And Filina, she just showed up?" Nandy stared at the empty platform.

"Yes." Rachel snuck a look at Pathik, remembering the night before. He hadn't made any mention of the fact she'd told Hannah she loved him.

The crowd noise swelled from a hum to buzz as David and Jim, the men who had helped abduct Rachel, stepped up onto the platform. As soon as they were both standing in the center the crowd went silent.

"Welcome to all." David spoke. "And may we celebrate another year tomorrow."

The crowd made approving noises.

"Today's assembly will be brief. We've much to do to prepare for Celebration." David smiled at the groans from various quarters. "I know, I know. But in order to feast we must cook!" He grew serious. "We have chosen our Honoree for the year."

More noise from the crowd, less jovial this time. Filina stepped up onto the platform and David and Jim stepped back, yielding their places as if she were royalty. She waited until there was silence in the cave.

"We have another announcement, before we name this year's Honoree." Filina surveyed the people, her expression neutral. "New community members are joining us today." She pointed to Rachel and the others in the group with no hesitation. She knew exactly where they were standing. "Come, please." She spoke the words as one accustomed to having her orders followed.

Rachel looked at her father. Some of her apprehension must have been visible on her face, because Daniel reached out and squeezed her hand. He bent toward her. "We're together," he whispered. "Don't worry." He turned to the rest of their group. "Ready?"

They moved together toward the platform. Rachel felt many eyes upon her. She tripped on something, some uneven section of ground and Pathik, who was right behind her, steadied her. He didn't let go of her hand again until they had all ascended the steps to the platform.

"Let me introduce our new friends." Filina's smile was wide, but it never reached her eyes.

Daniel stepped forward before she could say more. "I'd like to introduce us, if that's all right." He didn't wait for Filina's permission. "My name is Daniel." He looked down at all of the people who were looking back up at him. "This is my wife, Vivian." Daniel put his arm around Vivian and squeezed her shoulders. "My daughter, Rachel." Daniel nodded to Rachel to step forward, which she did. "Malgam, his partner, Nandy, his son, Pathik." Each stepped forward.

"We hope we'll be welcomed here. We hope to make a life with you—we've come a long way on that hope." He scanned the faces below him. "We're told we are your guests. That if we so choose, we can leave." Daniel waited, listening for a moment to see if any stray murmur contradicted this. The crowd was silent.

"That's not what we want. We want—we hope—to build lives here with you. We hope that we can learn from each other and prosper. We want to thank you all for the chance."

Rachel was gratified to hear sounds of approval from the crowd. She knew her father had taken a great risk, because she'd been watching Filina's face while he made his introduction. When Daniel had spoken about them being free to go, Filina's jaw had tightened, though she'd kept the smile frozen on her face. Rachel got the feeling she wasn't used to people speaking openly like that, nor did she like it. By doing it, Daniel had ensured that the terms of their stay as they understood them were broadcast to all.

"We . . ." Daniel's voice grew quiet. He stood frowning, saying nothing. Rachel watched as her mother took his hand and peered into his face.

"Daniel?" Vivian whispered her husband's name.

He shook his head. He turned and looked at Vivian as though he didn't know quite where they were, for just an instant. Then he smiled and readdressed the crowd. "Thank you. We just want to thank you all."

Filina floated forward and held up her hands, her lips still upturned in a stiff smile. "We welcome our new friends."

The crowd gave a smattering of applause.

Jim and David approached Daniel and the others, unobtrusively directing them off the platform. Once they were back down in the crowd, Filina signaled for silence from the people and they obliged quickly.

"And now, let's get to the purpose of our assembly today. Every year, careful consideration is given to the choice of Honoree. It is a great distinction—"

A murmur from the crowd rose up and Filina stared out, her eyes hard. The murmur faded.

"It is a great honor to be chosen, a chance to serve our community in a way that allows us to continue living here in safety."

"At what cost?" The cry came from far back in the crowd. Rachel searched the faces, trying to find the person who had spoken, but from her vantage point she couldn't see much. She thought it sounded like Tom's voice, but she could no longer see him, Hannah, or Hannah's family in the crowd.

Filina ignored the comment and continued. "As is our custom, we will announce this year's Honoree today. Tomorrow, at Celebration, we will feast, and commemorate our Honoree." Filina paused, allowing the tension of the moment to build. When she was satisfied that the crowd was waiting impatiently for her next words, she straightened her body like a dancer, head high. "This year's Honoree is . . . Hannah."

Rachel expected applause, or some sort of expression of approval from the crowd, and there was a smattering of clapping hands. But mostly there was silence.

"Hannah." Filina frowned, standing on the platform, waiting. "Come to the front and be recognized." She peered into the crowd looking for Hannah and when she had her in her sights, she stared, stared in such a way that Rachel felt a chill, watching it.

Rachel saw a box nearby, an old wooden crate of some sort, and she stepped up onto it in order to see past the crowd. She found Hannah's group and saw Tom, holding onto Hannah's wrist, pulling her back as she tried to move toward the platform. There were tear streaks on Tom's face and he was shaking his head, whispering urgently to Hannah, but she seemed oblivious to his pleas. Hannah's mother and father stood woodenly, wearing blank expressions. Polly looked from her parents to her sister to Tom, and soon enough, her own tears fell.

She joined Tom in trying to restrain Hannah from moving forward, but neither could stop her.

Rachel couldn't believe her eyes. Hannah didn't even look like herself, not the silly girl who'd fluttered around showing Rachel and Pathik the cave, not the older sister teasing Polly, not the shy lover glancing up at Tom. She was more an object than a person, moving with one goal, to do Filina's bidding and get to the platform. She broke free of the hands holding her back and walked toward the front of the crowd. Rachel watched, horrified, though she didn't know exactly why, as Hannah climbed the steps to the platform.

Filina smiled. She put a hand on Hannah's shoulder. At the same moment, Hannah's face cleared, and she looked surprised to find herself there, standing next to Filina, looking down at the crowd.

"Our brave Honoree, Hannah!" Filina squeezed Hannah's shoulder and Rachel could imagine the feeling of that hand, claw-like, on her own shoulder. Filina lifted her other hand to the crowd, encouraging them to applaud. They finally did. After a moment of applause, Filina took Hannah by the wrist and stepped back on the platform. Jim and David strode to the front of the platform and started handing out assignments.

Pathik took Rachel's hand and helped her down from the crate. He whispered to her, a worried look on his face. "Let's go find Tom"

Rachel nodded. "Let's tell them." She nodded toward their parents.

After a brief consultation, Rachel and Pathik set off. Daniel hadn't been happy to let them go, but Vivian, Malgam and Nandy had agreed they should try to find out more about what was going on. Nandy pointed out that the two had already been guests at Hannah's parents, so visiting now might seem less suspicious if it was just Rachel and Pathik. "Besides, we need to get back to the units. I bet Nipper's going crazy." Nandy had elected to leave the Woolly inside while they attended the assembly.

"We'll meet you back at the units in an hour." Pathik watched as the others headed away. "What did you think," he said, once they were out of earshot.

"Of Dad, or Hannah?" Rachel knew what he meant.

"Both." Pathik frowned. "It was like something was controlling them."

"Or someone." The image of Filina's face, of her staring at Hannah with such intensity, came back to Rachel. "Remember when you just got here, and we were all in the office?" She waited for Pathik's nod. "When I said they had Nipper—"

"Nandy just sat there." Pathik nodded again. "She would *never* have done that."

"Exactly." Rachel followed Pathik through what was left of the crowd. Most people had dispersed almost immediately after Hannah was announced as Honoree. "Filina said he was fine and Nandy just sat back down like she wasn't even worried." She didn't mention that she'd done the same thing earlier, when Filina had bid her to leave Nipper and go to the office.

"We need to find out what's going on here." Pathik quickened his pace.

When they arrived at Hannah's parents' unit, it appeared to be deserted. They knocked on the door, but no one came.

"You'd think there would be people here, friends celebrating Hannah being chosen as Honoree." Pathik knocked on the door again.

"I'm starting to think being chosen is not such a great thing." Rachel remembered Hannah, handing her the packet the night before. *It's me*, she'd said, as though who she was might disappear at any moment.

The unit door opened then, and Polly, eyes red, poked her head out. She stared at Rachel and Pathik, as though she didn't know who they were at first.

"Hello, Polly." Rachel spoke softly. "Are your parents here? Tom?"

Polly shook her head. "They went with Filina." She sniffed. "My parents did. They said they would be back soon. Tom—"

"I'm here." Tom slunk out from the shadows. "I was waiting for them to come back. Didn't expect you two." He hugged Polly when she ran to him. "It's all right Polly, it's going to be all right." Tom's face didn't match his words. "Let's go inside, where we can relax a little." He glanced around, looking uneasy.

They gathered in the front room, at the same table they'd had dinner at the night before. Rachel noticed that Tom locked the door. He sat down on one of the stools and opened his arms to Polly. She climbed up on his lap, the tears she'd been trying to hold back finally falling.

"You're all right. It's going to be all right." Tom held the child, rocking her gently.

"They said they'd try to get her back, Tom." Polly could barely get the words out. "They said they'd try, but Keith never came back." She looked up into Tom's face. "Hannah's not coming back either, is she?"

Tom shook his head. "We'll try, Polly." He lifted her up. "Time for you to take a nap now, so if we need you, you'll be strong." He carried Polly to the next room and Pathik and Rachel could hear the sounds of him tucking her into bed, trying to soothe her. Rachel didn't realize how upset she was until Pathik moved his stool closer to hers, put his arm around her waist.

"We'll find out what's going on." He smiled at her. "It'll be all right."

Rachel wanted, with everything she had, to believe him. But she didn't. She knew he didn't believe his reassurances, either, just from the look in his eyes.

Tom came back out to the main room. He sat down on his stool, slowly, as though he was an old, old man.

"She's sleeping." His voice was no more than a whisper. "She's worn out, poor thing. Worried to death about Hannah."

"Where *is* Hannah?" Pathik kept his voice low.

Tom stared at the table top. For a moment Rachel thought he hadn't heard Pathik, but then he looked up. "Right now, she's probably in the office. That's where they take them."

"The Honorees?" Rachel started to stand. "Let's go get her, then."

Tom slid his eyes Rachel's way. "It doesn't work like that. They'll just say she went willingly—*willingly*." He spat the word out with derision. "In front of all of us, today at assembly. You saw her." He sounded tired. "They'll wipe her sometime before tomorrow." His voice tore.

"Wipe her?" Pathik tightened his arm around Rachel's waist. He could feel the pain emanating from Tom; it was like a wave of red heat. "What does that mean?"

Tom focused on the table top again. "The Honoree thing only started a few years ago—" He counted on his fingers, matching something in his mind—Rachel realized it was the names of Honorees—with the number of fingers he ticked off. "It's been six years.

"Some people came to the island—they said they were from the government. I don't know which one." He squinted, as though it helped him remember. "I was on the beach that day, gathering clams like we used to do. I was just a kid then. Hannah was with me." He smiled. "She wasn't doing her fair share of the gathering, as usual. I think she knew I was sweet on her, even then." He sat, silent for so long that Rachel felt certain he'd forgotten they were even in the room.

"Tom," Rachel said, gently. "What happened?"

Tom's smile faded. He looked at her, and she could see how hard it was for him to bring himself back to the room they were in, how hard it was to let go of his memories of Hannah, that day on the beach.

"They came from nowhere." Tom frowned. "I didn't see a boat. I figured out later that they must have landed on some other beach on the island. They just appeared from behind the dune, at least twenty of them, all pointing guns. It was just us kids—Hannah, me, a couple of others. They grabbed Melissa, Hannah's friend. One of them said they'd kill us all if we gave them any trouble. They started dragging her away, but Melissa could ping—better than Hannah, stronger—and she did. Before they got far there were thirty, maybe forty of our people on the beach."

Tom closed his eyes. "Keith was there. He told them to let Melissa go, but they just laughed. Keith started toward the two men who had Melissa, and one of them pointed one of the strange guns at him and he fell. At first we all thought he was dead, but he was just asleep."

"The guns must have been stunners." Rachel wished they had one now. She thought of the stunner Ms. Moore had had, illegal, enough to get her sentenced to a Labor Pool if she'd been found with it her possession.

"I don't know." Tom continued. "Filina was there that day. She walked right up to them. It was the strangest thing. She just stared at them—the men holding Melissa—just stared, and talked softly. I couldn't hear what she was saying. But they let Melissa go."

Pathik and Rachel exchanged a look. "Filina was in charge back then, too?" asked Pathik.

Tom shook his head. "Nobody was in charge back then. It used to be different here. We all voted on things—at least the adults did. But that day, Filina was the only one who could stop them. Even though she *didn't* stop them, not really."

"She got Melissa back." Rachel said it grudgingly. She didn't like Filina.

Tom stared at her. "She didn't. After they gave Melissa back, she talked to them for a long time, on the beach. She told them they had to wait—that's all I really remember. She took Melissa away with her, somewhere. And when she came back she *gave* them Melissa. And she's given them another person every year since."

Chapter 11

He said they've been sending one person each year since that day on the beach. That girl, Melissa, was the first, and Keith, the man who carved all the newer units in the cave—that was his gift—was last year's Honoree." Pathik sounded sickened.

He and Rachel had returned to the units to tell the rest of the group what Tom had told them. Everyone was gathered around the table in the first unit.

"Tom thinks they wipe them—remove most of their memories—before they let them go, so they won't reveal the cave's location, or anything else the government wants to know. He said Melissa seemed different when she came back to the beach with Filina. Like she didn't really recognize him, or Hannah. He said all of the Honorees seem that way.

"They'd already been living here in the cave, but they started hiding it after Melissa got taken. They make sure that all the entrances are concealed, that no smoke is visible from their fires. There's a crude little village of shacks near one of the beaches—from the earliest days here—they've told the government people that's where they actually live.

"When it's time to hand over an Honoree, they have some sort of drop-point where they meet and the government takes the person away to the mainland." Pathik scowled. "Celebration is some strange way of honoring their lives before they get sent away."

"Who wipes them?" Malgam looked like he thought he already knew. "That Filina?"

Pathik shook his head. "Tom didn't say, but I don't think it's her. I don't know if they even actually do it—he may not know what he's talking about."

Rachel watched the oil lamp flicker in the center of the table. Her two orchid seedlings sat near it, tucked in their cubes, already looking paler in the dim light available to them in the cave. "They're going to die." She didn't realize she'd spoken aloud until she looked up to find all of them staring at her. "The orchids, I meant. There's no light in the cave."

Vivian turned to her daughter, a worried expression on her face. "We'll find them some daylight." She looked at the others one by one, first Nandy, then Malgam, Pathik, finally, Daniel. "Should we . . . should we leave? Try to find a different place on the island where we can make our own way? Indigo said it was a big place. Surely there's enough room—"

"We can't just walk away now." Daniel checked the door to the unit, ensuring it was shut tight. "We don't have supplies to last a week, and we don't know what these people will do if we try to leave. I don't even have a clear idea of where the exits to the cave are, because they blindfolded us in the tunnels. Do any of you?"

"They're just like the Roberts." Malgam practically snarled the words. "Trading their own for . . . for what?"

"We don't know enough to say that." Nandy put her hand on Malgam's. "It didn't look to me like everyone at assembly was onboard with Filina."

"Tom said he'd come let us know if Hannah's parents got her back." Pathik watched Rachel as he spoke. He'd been watching her since she said her orchids would die, a carefully neutral expression on his face. "He didn't think they'd have much luck."

"I guess we just wait, then?" Malgam shifted on his stool. The last thing he wanted to do was to wait.

Daniel nodded. "I don't think we have a lot of choice, right now. We'll see what news Tom brings. Until then, let's stick close to each other. Nobody leave the units alone. In fact, nobody leave the area, period."

Nandy, Malgam, and Nipper went to the second unit, Nandy making noises about Malgam needing rest, Malgam making noises about how he didn't. Daniel and Vivian remained in the first. Pathik and Rachel convinced the adults to let them sit just outside.

"It'll look more normal if we're not all huddled inside," said Pathik. "And we'll have a chance to watch, see what people are doing."

And so they sat, on a bench Pathik pulled up from one of the nearest work areas. Rachel thought there seemed to be less activity in the cave than normal, though as soon as she had that thought, she realized they'd been there too short a time to know what *normal* was. People were working, cooking, mending tools, but there was a tense feeling in the air. Nobody chattered back and forth, and everyone seemed to be avoiding eye contact.

"Cheerful bunch." Pathik said the words under his breath, without looking at Rachel.

"Yes." She didn't look at him either. "It's like . . ."

"Like they're ashamed." Pathik spat on the ground in front of him, something Rachel had never seen him do. "They *should* be, too."

One of the nearest workers—the same girl who had been sharpening knives before—looked up from her strop when Pathik spat. There was no glaring today. She glanced at Pathik, then at Rachel, and quickly lowered her eyes back to her work.

"I think Nandy might be right." Rachel watched the girl as she sharpened a pitted blade. "I think some of them aren't onboard with the whole thing."

"Then they should have stopped it."

Rachel thought about Nandy, sitting down in the office after she'd heard that Nipper was captive, about Daniel, stuttering on the platform at the assembly. She thought about Hannah, pulling away from Tom, walking like a robot up the stairs to Filina. She thought about the look on Filina's face, all those times. "They *should* have. I just wonder—"

"Company." Pathik nudged Rachel, a gentle warning.

Sarah strode up, her cheeks flushed. She stood in front of them, breathing fast as though she'd just been running. "Are your parents inside?"

"They are," said Rachel. Neither she nor Pathik moved from the bench.

"I need to see them." Sarah looked behind her at the people nearby, checking to see who was noticing. When she turned back, she took in Pathik's unimpressed expression and Rachel's stony gaze. "You don't have to like it. But I'm in a bit of a hurry."

"Feel free to knock." Pathik tilted his head toward the unit doors.

"I need to see the two of you, too." Sarah looked behind her again. "Now." She walked to the closest unit and tapped on the door. When it opened she didn't look back, she just disappeared inside.

"I'll get Malgam and Nandy." Pathik rose from the bench. "See you back inside."

Sarah waited until they were all assembled around the table again. She didn't sit with them. Instead, she stood near the door of the unit, tense, her arms crossed in front of her. When all eyes were on her, she spoke.

"We need your help."

There was silence from the table. Everyone stared up at Sarah; nobody said a thing. Finally, Malgam grunted. "What makes you think we're interested?" He narrowed his eyes, waiting for Sarah's response.

"You're all a part of this now." Sarah held Malgam's gaze. "And it needs to end."

"A part of what?" Daniel shifted on his stool so that he faced Sarah head on. "You might want to fill us in on what's going on if you want our help."

Sarah checked the door. She looked at each of them in turn, stopping at Rachel. "You've figured some of it out, I think."

Rachel nodded. "We know about Celebration." She stared at Sarah, her eyes dark. "We know about . . . Hannah."

"Then you know we need to stop it." Sarah's jaw tightened. "We need to stop Filina." She whispered the name, as though she feared someone outside might hear.

"You're asking us to help *you* stop Filina?" Pathik sounded incredulous. "You're one of her cronies, aren't you? You helped take Rachel, you were there in the office with Filina and her crew. Why would we help you?"

"More to the point, *how* could we help you?" Daniel cocked his head at Sarah. "What exactly do you think we could do that you can't? *You've* got numbers. If you don't like what Filina's doing, rise up and say so."

Sarah looked like she might cry. "You don't understand."

"I think I do," said Rachel. "Filina can control people. She can make them do what she wants." She looked at Sarah, eyes wide. "*That's* her talent, isn't it?"

Sarah nodded, silent.

Pathik watched Sarah's face. When he spoke his voice was pitiless. "Have you helped her? Have you ever amped her gift for her?"

Everyone waited to hear Sarah's answer, judgment building in each expression. Sarah bowed her head. She was silent for a long time. When she spoke, it was barely audible, just one word.

"Once."

Pathik hit the tabletop with his palms. "One time too many." His eyes burned with disgust.

"Wait." Nandy put a hand over one of Pathik's.

"What do you mean, wait?" Pathik shook her hand off. "That's against *all* that Indigo stood for, *all* that Usage means. It *matters* what we choose, it *matters*—"

"If we *can* choose." Nandy was watching Sarah, whose head was still bowed. A single tear slipped from Sarah's cheek and fell, hitting the floor. "Could you choose, that one time? Could you, Sarah?"

"What do you mean?" Vivian leaned forward toward Nandy, confused.

"*I* felt it. Filina's power." Nandy didn't take her eyes off Sarah. "When Rachel told me they had Nipper, I felt . . . slow. I didn't go to him. I stayed in that office." She turned to Malgam. "Is that what I would *ever* do?"

Daniel nodded. "I think I know what you mean. When we were on the platform, when I was speaking to the people. I think I felt it, too. I had more to say, but my mind felt—muddled. I just remember thinking I should be quiet. *I should be quiet, now.*"

Sarah looked up. "That's what she does. You forget. You forget what it was you wanted to do. You just *go along*, you do what she wants you to do. And later, when your mind is clear again, it's too late."

Malgam looked skeptical. "All right. So Filina is a mind-controller. And whatever she's got going with this Celebration thing—which we would need to know a lot more about—you want it to end. But you haven't answered Daniel's question. How can we help you? It's not like we're any more powerful than you are. We're just—what was it your friend—David—said? *Not very heavy hitters.* I believe he said all of us had rather crude gifts."

Sarah nodded. "He did say that."

"So what can we do to make any difference here at all?"

"It's not your talents that will help." Sarah

hesitated.

"Well, what *is* it then?"

Sarah took a breath. She looked sad, as though she didn't really want to say what she was about to say. But she said it.

"It's Rachel."

Chapter 12

Elizabeth dusted the last one of the china cups and set it back on the shelf with the rest of the dishes reserved for special occasions. They hadn't had one of those since Vivian and Rachel and the Others from Away had eaten here, before they all left to Cross. She smiled, remembering how astonished those two boys had been—Pathik and Fisher—at the hot running water and the abundance of food.

"I don't believe I've seen you dust since you were a little girl." Jonathan leaned on the door frame. He'd just returned from misting the orchids. He smelled like the greenhouse—like earth, and sun, and the perlite used in the potting mix.

"Mother always thought this sort of work was beneath us. When I was little, I loved it when the housekeeper would let me help, but that soon changed." Elizabeth shook her head. "I guess I became a lot more like Mother than I ever meant to be."

Jonathan grunted. "You're not so like her if I remember her correctly." He tilted his hat back off his forehead and changed the subject. "No sign of any EOs this morning."

Since the man from the government had paid his chilling visit, they'd both been nervously watching the road, dreading the daily EO drive-by. They came slowly down the long lane, crawling past the house, making certain that Elizabeth and Jonathan saw them. The officers always remained in the vehicle, staring from the windows.

"So far." Elizabeth sighed. "They'll be by. They want us to know they're watching."

Jonathan nodded. "Do you think I could talk you into a cup of kalitea? I'm ready for a break already today. Getting old."

Elizabeth smiled. "I'm ready for a break, too, after just doing the dusting. We're both getting old, I think."

When they'd readied the kalitea—a comfortable, silent routine consisting of Jonathan brewing the tea while Elizabeth took down mugs, sugar and cream—they settled in the parlor. Elizabeth was glad Jonathan had asked for kalitea; she had something on her mind. After they'd each had a few sips, she set her mug down.

"I think we may need to get out those books you had—the ones about Salishan."

Salishan was one of the relinquished islands—the ones that had been left out of Unifolle's Border Defense System. It had been too expensive to include them, so the government had evacuated the inhabitants instead, and now the islands were abandoned. Radiation from the bombs dropped in a long-ago attack made it unsafe—according to the government—for anyone to set foot on the islands.

There had always been rumors that some people weren't evacuated, that they may have survived the bombings. But those were just whispers, like the whispers about the territory Away. When Rachel and the Others had Crossed, Jonathan had researched Salishan, hoping to draw Elizabeth out of the fog of grief she'd wandered in since Indigo's death. He'd been careful to stay off the Net, so finding information had been difficult, but he had found some books.

Jonathan and Elizabeth thought Salishan was the island Indigo had talked about, the one Rachel and the Others would go to, if they could. They had read all they could find about it, and pondered various, impossible routes to its shores. But Elizabeth had finally asked Jonathan to put the books away. She was tired of dreaming.

"Are you thinking we need to make a move?" Jonathan didn't sound surprised.

Elizabeth frowned. "I don't know how we even *could*. But it can't help to know the specifics, can it?"

Jonathan stared into his mug. He started to speak, but stopped himself. He took a sip of his tea instead. Elizabeth watched, letting seconds tick by, until she couldn't wait any longer.

"What is it?" She said the words gently. She knew she was sharp with Jonathan far too often, and she felt bad about it. She and he shared so many years, so many secrets. So much pain.

"I . . ." Jonathan set his mug down, carefully. "I was assuming a bit much I guess, to ask if you were thinking *we* should make a move." He kept his eyes on the table.

Elizabeth watched his face, looking for traces of anger, but there were none. She saw only sadness, sadness she knew she had caused. "Of course it would be *we*, Jonathan."

He looked up then, meeting her gaze with a quiet dignity. There was no gratitude in his eyes, and Elizabeth realized there shouldn't be. He was his own person. He was here with her because he chose it, even after all she'd put him through. *She* should be grateful, if anyone should. She waited to see what he would say. When he spoke, he didn't mention all that had passed between them in the last moments. He was exactly Jonathan: practical.

"I'll go get the books."

Chapter 13

"Rachel?" Everyone in the unit said Rachel's name with different degrees of surprise, except for Pathik. He said her name softly, not surprised at all, only fear and resignation coloring his voice.

Sarah noticed his reaction. She watched Pathik as the others began to ask their questions.

"What can Rachel do against Filina?" Vivian sounded panicked.

"She doesn't even have a gift." Malgam pronounced the words like a verdict.

Daniel put his arm around Vivian's trembling shoulders. He leveled his gaze at Sarah. "I think you'd better explain what you have in mind."

Sarah looked from Pathik to Daniel. "I will." She pulled the last stool from the corner of the room to the table and sat down on it. "I think Rachel may be the only person who can help us win against Filina."

"Why?" Malgam frowned. "Filina has a powerful gift from what you say. Rachel has nothing."

Sarah watched as Nandy stroked Nipper's head, calming the Woolly, who had become alert to the tension in the room. "Talents—gifts—exist in many different forms."

"She thinks I can resist Filina." Rachel spoke quietly, directing her words to Pathik as though there was nobody else in the room. She waited, as though she'd asked him a question. After a long silence, Pathik nodded. His eyes were shining in the low light from the lamp.

"But I can't. When I found Nipper in the cage, when I wanted to stay with him, protect him, I went along with her instead." Rachel turned to Sarah. "Remember? I followed Filina like a puppy, as soon as she told me to do it."

"I do remember." Sarah smiled at Rachel. "The thing you don't realize is that you *didn't*. You didn't do what she said to right away. She had been trying to make you go with her from the minute she walked up to you, but you resisted. I saw it. She really had to work to get you to go. The only other person I've *ever* seen who could resist her even a tiny bit was Keith, and he's gone now. You're our best chance. Our only chance."

Rachel didn't look convinced. "Even if I can resist her, what good does that do us?"

"Tomorrow, during Celebration, you can expose her." Sarah saw the look on Rachel's face and held up her hand. "More and more of the people out there are beginning to doubt Filina, doubt the whole idea of Honorees. They don't know, most of them, exactly what happens to an Honoree—all they know is that some sort of arrangement has been made, that if we give the government one person a year they'll leave us alone."

Pathik spoke. "What *does* happen to the Honorees?"

"And which government is it Filina's dealing with?" Daniel leaned back. "Given the location of this island, I'd say it's either the Unified States or Unifolle."

"What difference does any of that make?" Vivian glared at Sarah. "Rachel's not doing anything for you. If Filina can just control everyone except for Rachel, why wouldn't she just make them think Rachel was lying if she exposed her? Why wouldn't she turn the rest of your people against her?"

"It doesn't work that way." Sarah sounded frustrated. "Filina can't control everyone all at once. She can send out a wide-range suggestion, but it's weak compared to when she focuses on a single person."

"She did that yesterday, didn't she? Sent out a suggestion?" Nandy kept stroking Nipper, who had tensed again at Vivian's outburst. "When the crowd started getting loud at assembly, and then suddenly they quieted down."

Sarah nodded. "Yes. But she can't *really* control a crowd, like I said. She can only suggest something and hope it takes. And there are those of us who will be ready for that, ready to take action if things get out of hand. We'll have surprise on our side." She looked at Daniel. "In answer to your question, it's the Unified States taking the Honorees. I heard Filina telling Keith when this all first started."

"Keith was last year's Honoree, wasn't he?" Pathik looked gratified at Sarah's evident surprise that he knew this. "Are you going to tell us what happened to him, what happened to the others before him?"

Sarah bowed her head. For a long moment she was silent. When she spoke, it sounded as if each word caused her physical pain. "Keith had been arguing with Filina more and more about the Honoree system. He thought we should stop sending people, thought Filina should tell everyone what was going on so we could all decide what to do."

"What do the rest of the people *think* is going on every year when you ship off one of your own to the government?" Malgam folded his arms and cocked his head dubiously at Sarah.

"Everyone knows we have an agreement, but nobody knows the details. They just know that a person is picked by the council each year and sent to the mainland. 'Fostering relations' is how Filina puts it. It's considered a distinction for the Honoree, a brave sacrifice to preserve our freedom.

"They don't know that there *is* no real council vote. Filina picks the Honoree—someone with inconsequential talent who matches the general requirements they asked for that year." Sarah nodded at their surprised looks. "Keith told me they send a list each year, with guidelines for what they want the next year. Filina always picked someone who matched their requirements but who didn't have an incredibly powerful talent. Pingers, movers, as long as they couldn't move much. That sort of thing." She sighed. "Anyway. Keith only knew all this because he was on the beach that day, the day the first government men showed up and tried to take Melissa. He was there when Filina made the deal. He saw how frightened Melissa was when they tried to take her. He saw how changed she was when Filina returned with her and gave her to them. He said it was like she was sleep-walking."

Sarah squeezed her eyes shut, but a tear escaped. "None of them have come back, even though they're supposed to return them before they get someone new. Every year, the men from the government tell Filina that whoever went last decided they'd rather stay, that they'd rather live on the mainland. Who wouldn't, they say, when life here is so hard, so crude." Sarah wiped her eyes with the backs of her hands.

"I think Filina actually believed it for a while, but Keith never did. I don't believe it either. I think . . . I'm afraid something terrible has happened to them."

"What about last year?" Nandy asked the question as gently as she could. "Why did Filina choose Keith as Honoree?"

"As I said, Keith had been pushing harder and harder to stop sending Honorees. He'd argued and argued with Filina, but she kept telling him it was our only hope, that the government would just eradicate us if we didn't work with them. She insisted that the secrecy about what they were actually doing with them was necessary, that the people didn't have the stomach to do what had to be done to save us. She talked about it being a small sacrifice for the greater good." Sarah's lip curled.

"He planned to expose her himself, to bring it all out in the open so the people could decide what we should do. But she suspected. At assembly last year, she announced his name as Honoree. She must have got lucky in terms of him matching what they requested."

"But why did he go?" Vivian was watching Rachel, as though she feared the girl would disappear right before her eyes. "If he could resist Filina's power, why didn't he go ahead and expose her anyway?"

Sarah took a deep, shuddering breath. Her tears fell unchecked. She tried to answer, but a sob caught her, wracked her. All she could do was shake her head.

"That was the one time, wasn't it?" Nandy whispered the words. "The one time you amped for Filina. She turned her power on you, first, so that she could overcome Keith's resistance."

A fresh round of sobs overcame Sarah. She stared at Nandy, trembling. A slight incline of her head told the tale.

Nandy put her hand on Sarah's shoulder and pressed down gently, as though she were afraid Sarah might fly away in her pain. "You couldn't help it. She made you do it."

Sarah's face crumpled. She tried to say something, and choked on her tears instead.

Pathik didn't seem moved by her pain. "You say Keith knew all this because he was there on the beach that day. He could resist Filina somehow, or at least try, and she had to take him into her confidence." He studied her. "But you weren't there, were you? How do you know all this? She can just make you do what she wants—she doesn't have to fill you in on the details. So why are you privy to Filina's schemes? Unless it's because you're on her side."

After a moment, Sarah was able to speak. What she said sent a chill through all of them. "Keith is my father."

Chapter 14

Hours later, after plans had been made, after Sarah had slipped back out the door, the group still sat, exhausted, around the table. Light from the lamp flickered, casting ominous shadows. Rachel's orchid seedlings looked shriveled in their cubes, rubbery and pale.

"Can you imagine," said Vivian, "being forced to act against your own father that way?"

"If she's telling us the truth, he's probably in some lab somewhere on the mainland, with electrodes hooked up everywhere they can think to attach them. Either that or dead, by now." Malgam looked grim. "It's disgusting."

"The way she said Keith acted on his Celebration day, like he didn't even know her. And Hannah, giving Rachel her mementos in case she was chosen as Honoree." Nandy shook her head. "It's more than just controlling them so they act like they want to be Honorees. I think Tom's theory about wiping memories must be true." She sighed. "I wonder how Filina is doing that."

Pathik caught Rachel's eye and tilted his head slightly toward the door. "I'm going to sit outside for a while."

"I'll come, too." Rachel smiled at Vivian's expression. "It's okay, Mom. We'll be right outside on the bench."

"Don't wander off." Vivian tried to smile back at her daughter, but her lips remained pressed together in a tight line.

Outside the unit, Pathik sat down on the rough bench and patted the spot next to him. He leaned forward, elbows on thighs, hands dangling between his knees, staring out toward the cave's central area. People moved about, doing the things they did to keep the camp going. Someone baked bread, someone watched children, someone else repaired a table, winding twine around a loose joint.

"It looks like it could be a good place, doesn't it?" Rachel sounded wistful.

"Are you going to do it?" Pathik didn't look at her.

Rachel followed his gaze to the group of children, who were being given some sort of lesson.

It looked like the youngest ones were learning the names of colors, while older ones were learning to spell the names. "It seems like it could work." She'd been thinking, ever since Sarah laid out the plan, about how it could work even better.

"We could just go back. We could try to make it work Away."

Rachel laughed, a gentle laugh. "How would we do that? We lost the boat."

"I bet they have a boat, somewhere."

"You don't want to go back there, do you?" Rachel waited, watching Pathik. "You wanted something better. So did Indigo. This could be it."

"I don't want you in danger." Pathik still didn't look at her. "I—" He swallowed. "I keep thinking about that first night. If I hadn't come to you for help, if I'd never asked you to get the medicine—"

"Malgam would be dead. And we'd never have met." Rachel remembered that night, the shape coming toward her in the dark, from the other side of the Line. How the shape turned into a boy, how the boy turned into Pathik. The magic feeling of seeing someone across the Line, someone from Away.

"You wouldn't be in any danger, either."

"There are all kinds of danger." Rachel thought about her life on The Property, always hiding, staying out of trouble, never really free. She was afraid to do what Sarah suggested, afraid Filina would find a way to control her, to stop her. But she knew she had to be brave. "Do you believe I can resist Filina?"

Pathik sat up straight. Then he turned to her, his blue eyes shining. "It sounds like you already have." He studied her face as though he were memorizing it. "If anyone could, it would be you."

"Why do you say that?" Rachel didn't like how sad he looked just then.

"You've always . . . you've always sort of known, haven't you, what's right and what's wrong. And you've always had the strength to do the first one. To actually *do* it, Rachel, not just know the difference." He smiled. "That's a huge thing. It's a thing that takes such courage." He looked down at his feet. "I've always loved that about you, and sometimes, I've wondered if I can keep up." His voice became a whisper. "Actually *doing* the right thing is so hard. Sometimes, I'm . . . I'm afraid to do the right thing."

Rachel laughed. "Do you think I'm not afraid?"

Pathik looked up at her. "Are you?"

"Every time. Sometimes I think I'm afraid *most* of the time."

"You seem so brave."

Rachel had to laugh again. "You know what Ms. Moore told me once? She said, in order to be brave, you *have* to be afraid. Otherwise you're not really being brave."

Pathik thought about that. "She was pretty smart, wasn't she?"

Rachel's smile fell away. "I miss her."

Pathik looked out at the people in the cavern. He watched the woman who was fixing the table as she coated the twine repair with some sort of tarlike substance. "She reminded me a lot of Indigo. I can see why they fell in love." He scowled. "I wish she'd come with us. I wonder what she'd think of this place."

Rachel knew Pathik would have liked both of them, Indigo *and* Ms. Moore, to come. She knew he'd always blame himself for Indigo's death, for Ms. Moore staying behind. "She stayed because it gave us a chance to get away, Pathik, it gave us some time. The government was watching The Property—if she'd turned up missing they would have been after us all so fast, we'd never have made it Away."

"She wouldn't have stayed, if Indigo had been alive to make her come. Besides, what good did it do us, really, to get away? We just ended up here, where they *still* fear the government."

Rachel reached out her hand, waiting until Pathik saw it. When he took it in his, she smiled. "I have an idea, Pathik."

The group spent the rest of the day trying to act normal. Tom came by to say that Hannah's parents had had no luck in retrieving their daughter. When they'd banged on the office door, Filina's lackey David had told them Hannah was fine, that they would see her at Celebration before she left, that they knew how these things worked. When they'd protested, he'd simply shut the door in their faces. Hannah's mother was hysterical and Hannah's father was trying to comfort her and Polly back at their unit.

Tom looked as grim as a person could look. Rachel suspected he was thinking about Hannah being wiped. She stole a glance at Pathik, wondering what it would be like if he suddenly stopped being *him*, with all his irritating habits, all his singular traits. What if he stopped doing all the things that made her love him? What if all his memories of her disappeared?

"Have you seen Sarah, Tom?" Malgam asked the question cautiously; he didn't know how much Tom knew about the plan, or if he knew about it at all.

Tom was equally cautious. "Why would I?" He frowned at Malgam. "She's one of Filina's crew. I have no reason to see her."

Malgam raised his eyebrows.

"No reason at all." Tom was practically stuttering.

Malgam shot Daniel a look. Daniel nodded.

"What?" Tom held his hands up and shrugged.

Malgam stretched, raising his arms over his head languorously. "You're not so great at lying." He was about to add something when they all heard a tap at the unit door. Pathik opened the door a crack, then wide, and Sarah entered.

"Tom!" She looked annoyed. "I've been looking everywhere for you. We told you to meet us at—"

"I don't know what you mean." Tom made a stiff movement with his head, angling it toward Malgam and Daniel. "I have no reason to meet you anywhere." He jerked his head again, eyes wide.

"Tom." Sarah put her hands on her hips. "They know."

Tom's eyes got even wider. "What? What do they know?"

"I told them. Everything. They're going to try to help us." Sarah looked at Rachel. "I think."

Rachel couldn't help but to smile at Tom's dumbfounded expression. She nodded to him. "It's okay, Tom. We have a sort of plan." She caught Pathik's eye, but looked away before anyone else noticed.

An hour later, Tom and Sarah left, off to finalize the parts of the plan they could. Rachel and the rest of her group were ready for a quick dinner, which they shared around the table in the first unit. After that, Malgam, Nandy and Pathik retired to their unit. The morning would come sooner than any of them wanted it.

Rachel slipped into the bedroom before her parents went to bed. She needed to find the waterproof bag that held Vivian's portfolio, and she needed to do it without Vivian or Daniel finding out. She rummaged through the scant supplies that had survived the boat wreck and finally found what she was looking for. Her hands trembling, she drew out the maps. Relics from the collaboration, the resistance movement her mother and father had been a part of in the Unified States—the maps had been passed from member to member, carefully guarded, hidden away for future use. All those years that she and her mother had lived quietly on The

Property, thinking her father was dead, the maps had been in the portfolio along with other contraband documents. She barely had time to hide them in her pocket when Vivian came in.

"What are you doing?" Vivian looked worried. Rachel wasn't in the habit of digging around in her mother's things, certainly not in the portfolio.

"I . . . I was hoping you might have a pen and some paper in here." Rachel held her breath, feeling horrible for the lie she was about to tell.

"What for?"

"I know that it will be fine tomorrow." Rachel didn't have to feign her apprehension. "I just wanted—I mean if something goes wrong. I wanted to write some things down."

Vivian furrowed her brow. "Like what, Rachel?"

"Like, well, like Hannah did, for Tom."

Vivian came to her and hugged her, holding her so tight Rachel had to loosen her hold in order to breathe. "Rachel. Nothing's going to go wrong." Vivian smoothed Rachel's hair back from her forehead. "Are you afraid we'd forget who you are? Like Hannah was afraid?"

Rachel shook her head. "I know you wouldn't. I wanted to write a letter for Pathik." Rachel couldn't stop the flush that came into her cheeks. She knew her mother was aware that she and Pathik had feelings for each other, but actually talking about it with her was uncomfortable.

Vivian peered at her daughter for a moment, smiling. "Ah. I see." She picked up the portfolio.

"Well, it just so happens you're in luck." She unzipped a side pocket and produced three sheets of printer paper and a pen. "I guess my over-organized self is looking pretty good now, isn't it?"

Rachel smiled. "I always did give you a hard time about your rules, didn't I?"

"A hard time? I'd say that was an understatement." Vivian tried to look stern, but her eyes were twinkling. "I love you, Rachel. And so does your father. You know that, right?"

Rachel hugged Vivian tight, as tight as her mother had hugged her a moment ago. She hid her face, because if Vivian saw it, she would know something was not right. "I love you both, too."

Vivian held her for a moment more. "Send your father in here for me. We'll turn in so you can have some privacy in the main room. But don't stay up writing for too long."

With a last look over her shoulder, Rachel left her mother and went out to get Daniel.

He was still sitting at the table, looking weary. The shadows from the oil lamp deepened the darkness under his eyes. When he saw Rachel, his face lightened some, and he smiled.

"Mom's ready for bed." Rachel stood looking at him. She was still amazed to see him sometimes—breathing, moving, talking—her dead father, come back to life.

"You ready, too? Is that cot treating you all right?" Daniel nodded toward the cot in the corner of the room.

"It's not too bad."

Daniel slowly pulled himself up from his stool. "I feel like I might actually creak, if I'm not careful." He smiled ruefully.

Rachel hugged him then, holding him tight, feeling his strength and solidness. He was such a good man, such a good father. She wondered how much she'd missed, not having him all those years he'd been gone. "I love you, Dad."

Daniel hugged her back. He didn't say a word, not for the longest time. But then he held her away from him and looked at her with such deep emotion he couldn't speak for a moment. When he did, his voice was tight. "I love you too, Rachel. I've loved you since the day you were born. Through all the years, even when I wasn't with you, I thought of you. You and your mother kept me alive through some bad times."

"Better get some rest now." Rachel felt . . . too much. She didn't want the morning to come, but she knew it would.

"Morning's coming no matter what." Daniel spoke as though he had read her mind. "I guess we'd all better sleep."

Once she was certain her parents were asleep, Rachel took the maps out and carefully smoothed them flat on the table. She wasn't sure which map might be the best one to use. After a while, she decided any one would do and just picked the one on the top of the stack. She placed a sheet of the blank paper her mother had given her over the map, and in the dim light, her eyes heavy, she began to trace.

In the second unit, Malgam and Nandy slept in the bedroom. Pathik sat at the table, turning an envelope over and over in his hands. His name was written on the envelope, in a scrawled cursive. There was a letter in the envelope, a letter from his grandmother, Elizabeth Moore, written to him before she ever met him, before she knew she ever would. Rachel had given it to him when she first Crossed, when they'd first begun to know one another. She'd had two others, one for his father, Malgam, and one for his grandfather, Indigo. He knew they'd both read their letters, though they hadn't shared what was in them.

Pathik had kept his, sealed in its envelope, through all that had happened since Rachel had handed it to him. He wasn't sure why he hadn't opened it. He'd come close many times, especially once he'd actually met his grandmother. But somehow, it always felt better to keep the envelope sealed. As if keeping it sealed kept something from ending—something he didn't want to end.

Tonight, he felt differently. He thought maybe keeping the envelope sealed kept something from beginning. Something he might have been afraid of before. He didn't feel as afraid now.

He made a small tear at the top of the envelope, and wiggled his finger inside. Then he pushed along the fold, ripping the envelope open wide. There was a single sheet inside and he could see there was very little written on that sheet. He unfolded it, wondering if he was about to be disappointed.

Pathik.

I'm told that's your name.

What can I say to you, my grandson, when I've only seen you once, darting back into the grass like a wild animal. Knowing, my child, that I helped to put you there, in that horrible place. Afraid. Alone. Yet, I saw courage in you. I saw hope. More than I've ever had, though the fault's mine.

Let me tell you about love, Pathik. I know about it now, now when it's too late. Love is all that matters, my boy. Remember that. Love is pain. Love is fear. But love is all that matters, in the end.

Don't lose love because of the pain, or the fear. Do what needs to be done, whatever that is, to keep your love alive. That's all I know, and it may be all any of us needs to know.

Your grandmother, who misses all that she lost,

Elizabeth Moore

Pathik read the letter twice. Then, he folded it carefully and replaced it in its envelope. He put the envelope in his pocket.

He didn't feel disappointed.

Chapter 15

Hannah wasn't certain if it was still evening or if it was the middle of the night—it wasn't possible to tell in the cave, where the light never changed. She only knew it was late. She'd been locked in the small room off the office since morning, when her name had been announced as Honoree.

She didn't remember much about the morning except how afraid she'd been. She was afraid while she got dressed. Afraid while Tom tried to talk her out of going to assembly, which hadn't worked, of course. She knew they'd never get away, at least not far enough. And if they did manage to get out, she knew Filina would make her family pay for it, somehow. Maybe she'd make sure Polly was Honoree when she was old enough. Hannah couldn't take that chance, no matter how much Tom pleaded.

She remembered being afraid while they walked to her parents' unit to meet them, afraid while Polly showed her the new doll her father had carved her from a small piece of driftwood. She'd felt sad at how her father and mother were acting—excited—as though it would be a great thing if she was named Honoree. They still believed the fairytale Filina had spun for the people.

She remembered being afraid right up until the moment after she heard her name. After that, all she could recall was a fog, a gray fuzzy feeling in her mind as she walked, oddly compelled, toward where Filina stood up on the platform. Then, nothing.

Nothing at all, until about an hour ago. She'd suddenly come to, as if she'd been in a trance of some sort before. When she did, all she saw was the small room, the locked door, the bowl of stew someone left for her, cold and congealing on the table. She felt tired, as though she'd been awake for many hours.

This must be the place they had all come before her, all of the previous Honorees. Hannah didn't know exactly what happened; nobody did. She only knew that during Celebration, family and close friends were able to visit the Honoree briefly before they went away. They must do it here, in this tiny room. She wondered how long until her mother and father, Tom and Polly, maybe Gina, her closest friend, would be allowed to see her one last time.

She thought about the girl, Rachel. The girl from Away. She hoped Rachel knew how important the packet she'd given her was—how much was sewn inside that scrap of fabric. She hoped Tom wouldn't be too sad when he read the letter she'd written to him. She hoped he'd think of her when—

Hannah felt her hands tightening into fists. She looked down at them as though they weren't *her* hands at first, but soon enough she felt the strength in them traveling up her arms, into her shoulders, through her chest. She would not succumb to this. No. She would fight. When that door opened, she would be ready. If Filina thought she would just go quietly along with whatever was planned, she had a big surprise coming. Hannah would fight and she would find her way back to Tom.

She didn't have long to wait. The door latch creaked upward and then the door swung out. Hannah watched as Filina stepped into the room. The woman looked tired, more tired than Hannah had ever seen her look. There were circles under her eyes, and she moved as though her body ached.

"Time to go now, Hannah." Filina barely looked at her.

Hannah didn't move.

"I said, time to go." Filina sounded as tired as she looked. When Hannah didn't respond to her command, she sighed. "*Now*, girl. I don't have time for this."

"Is that the way you talked to the other

Honorees?" Hannah snorted. "Not very respectful of those who are making *such great sacrifices for our people.*" She made her voice important and formal when she spoke, mocking the way Filina always said the same words at assembly. She wasn't sure where she got the courage to speak this way to Filina—the woman who led them all now, the woman many feared, including Hannah, without really knowing why. All she knew was that she wanted Tom. She just wanted to get back to Tom. "I'm not going anywhere." She jutted her chin up and out, hoping she looked braver than she felt.

Filina just stared at her. Hannah felt something tug at her thoughts, muddling them, swirling them around into a nebulous mist. She found herself standing. She took a step toward Filina.

"Everything all right here?" Jim, who'd heard Hannah's outburst leaned in the doorway.

At the sound of his voice Hannah felt herself snap back, clarity sharpening her thoughts once again. She stumbled backwards. "I'm not going." Her voice trembled with effort.

"We don't have time for this." Filina looked at Jim. "I'll be busy with Lethe. I can't be worried about Hannah."

Jim frowned. "Should I doze her?" Usually they went willingly.

Filina gave him a look of contempt. "Yes, Jim. Do I need to spell everything out for you?"

"Sorry." Jim stepped all the way into the room and closed the door. He leaned his back against it; there was no space for him to stand anywhere else in the small room. Hannah shrank away from him, but she couldn't escape his talent. Within seconds she slumped to the floor, unconscious.

"Get David and have him help you take her to Lethe's." Filina dismissed Jim without another glance. She stopped as she opened the door to leave, though, and looked down at Hannah. "Better tie her up." Then, she left.

Hannah awoke in another room she didn't recognize. It looked like the main room of any unit, with one door leading to a bedroom, another to a bathroom. There were signs that someone lived here; a box of toys that reminded her of Polly sat in a corner. A jar on the table held some sea glass—Hannah remembered gathering smooth, pastel pieces of it from the beach, wetting the sugared surfaces with her tongue to see the colors deepen.

Filina sat at the table. She was watching Hannah; she must have been waiting for her to regain consciousness. Hannah jerked up on the cot she was laying on, trying to stand, but her limbs were bound. She stared at the twine wrapped around her wrists, hope dying in her chest. She looked up at Filina, who still sat, quietly watching her.

"What happens now?" Hannah hated herself for the quaver in her voice.

"Now we get you ready to go." Filina sounded completely exhausted.

"Mother?" A girl, not much older than Polly, emerged from the bedroom doorway. She was holding a cloth doll. He face was round and fat-cheeked, sweet as anything Hannah had seen. "Is this her?" The girl nodded toward Hannah.

"Yes, Lethe." Filina's voice took on a gentle quality. "This is her. Her name is Hannah."

"And she's very sad?" The girl tilted her head.

"Yes." Filina sighed. "She's very sad and she needs you to help her. Like you did the others."

Lethe walked over to where Hannah lay on the cot. She regarded Hannah shyly. "I'm sorry you're so sad. Do you want to forget? Will it make you feel better?"

Hannah struggled to sit up. Lethe carefully set her doll on the edge of the cot and took Hannah's arm, helping her. She patted Hannah's shoulder. "It will be all right. Don't worry." She sounded just like Polly did when she was playing doctor.

"Who are you?" In the cave, everyone knew everyone and Hannah didn't think she'd seen this girl before. She'd called Filina *Mother*, but Hannah knew Filina was childless. "Who is she?" Hannah didn't really expect Filina to answer.

"This is Lethe." Filina still spoke gently.

"I came from the ocean." Lethe spoke the words like they were the beginning of a story, one someone had read to her many times.

"You came from the ocean and now you're mine." Filina held out her hands, and Lethe ran to her. She wrapped her arms around Filina and hugged her.

"And I help people who are sad."

"Yes, you do, Lethe." Filina hugged the child

back. She stared at Hannah over Lethe's shoulder, her eyes dispassionate. "You can help Hannah, too."

"I don't need any help!" Hannah was shaking with anger, but she couldn't stop the tears welling up in her eyes. "I need to go home!"

Lethe unwrapped herself from Filina's embrace and turned to face Hannah. Her lower lip trembled and her voice wavered when she spoke. "She's saying it, too, Mother. You said they don't want to remember their homes, but she's saying it too, just like the man did." She put her thumb in her mouth, sucking anxiously.

Filina took hold of Lethe's shoulders and turned the girl to face her. She smoothed the hair back from Lethe's forehead and murmured to her. "Sometimes people don't know what's best for them, Lethe. We talked about this. Sometimes you have to help them even when they don't think you're helping." Her eyes grew sharp and she focused on the little girl's face. "Help Hannah now, Lethe. Help her to forget."

Lethe swayed a bit, and when she turned to look at Hannah there was a blank quality in her gaze. She pulled her thumb just far enough out of her mouth to speak. "I'll help you, Hannah. Don't worry."

Hannah shook her head, sobbing. She knew what was going to happen. She'd heard the rumors, the whispers from family members about how past Honorees didn't recognize them during the last visit, how they didn't know anything about the cave, or the community. Somehow, this strange little girl was the cause of it. It must be her talent. What a horrible thing, to have been born with that as your talent, Hannah thought. There had been times when she'd wished she could do more than ping, when she'd wanted something flashy as her talent, something like fire-starting or stone carving, but she couldn't imagine having the sort of power Lethe had, couldn't imagine wanting it.

Hannah squeezed her eyes shut and thought of Tom, picturing his face in her mind, his smile, his eyes, the bump on his nose. She concentrated hard, holding on as tight as she could to his image. She peeked at Lethe, who was still standing before her, sucking her thumb. When she closed her eyes again, Tom's image was fainter. Something about his eyes was less . . .Tom. Hannah whimpered. She tried to imagine exactly how he looked, but the image just got hazier. She thought of Polly, of her mother and father, of their homey front room. Pictures appeared in her mind and faded. She couldn't hold on to any of them long—they slipped away like time.

Later, Hannah became aware of someone humming, softly, tunelessly. She opened her eyes and saw a girl standing in front of her, a little girl, holding a doll and humming. The girl peered at her and smiled.

"Are you happier now?"

Hannah frowned. She didn't know what the girl meant. She looked past the girl and saw a man and a woman talking at the table. They noticed her, but they didn't get up. The little girl held her doll out to

Hannah.

"Do you want to play for a while?" The girl seemed so hopeful, Hannah couldn't say no.

Jim shook his head. "It's eerie how they do that." He kept his voice low. David had left as soon as they'd carried Hannah in, but he'd stayed to take the girl back to the office. It seemed like it was always his job—escort them here, escort them back.

"Do what?" Filina sounded distracted.

"Just . . . change. Forget. And they don't even know it." Jim had to suppress a shudder.

"Yes, well. It's lucky for us. For all of us. That child is a gift to us." She moved the oil lamp slowly back and forth between her hands, sliding it along the surface of the table.

"But what she takes." Jim didn't look convinced that Lethe was such a gift.

"She can take. But she can give back, too. It's just . . . there's been no call for that." Filina thought about that. The ones who were supposed to come back. The ones who never did. She shook the thought off. There was nothing to be done about it. "After you take Hannah back to the office I need you to check on Sarah."

"Sarah?" Jim frowned. "Why?"

Filina didn't look up from the lamp. "I just want to know where she is, what she's up to tonight. Tomorrow we have to be prepared. Those new people—I don't like how they're acting. And nothing can go wrong with the transport. I might need her."

Jim shrugged. "She invited me to dinner tonight, so checking on her should be pretty easy." He'd had an eye on Sarah for a year or so, had hoped her dinner invitation was a sign that she might be feeling the same way, until he learned that several people had been invited. Still, he was pleased to be among them. It was a start. Sarah was a fine woman, and now that her father was gone, she needed to settle down, make a home with someone. "I'm sure if you need her she'll be there for you."

"I'm *not* sure, Jim." Filina's voice was razor-sharp. "So do as I ask. Sniff around, see if anything seems amiss."

Jim lowered his eyes. "Fine." He stood. "I'll get her back to the office now." He walked over to Hannah and Lethe and bent down, speaking to Hannah where she sat on the cot, watching Lethe play with her doll. "We need to go to another place, now." He took her hand and helped her up. "You can sleep there tonight, and tomorrow some people will come visit you."

Hannah just nodded. She felt tired. Sleeping sounded like a good thing.

Filina sat next to Lethe's bed, watching the child breathe. She should go. Jim had left an hour ago, and she had things to do to prepare for Celebration. But watching Lethe was peaceful, and she craved that peace. She could still see Lethe as a toddler, wandering alone on the far beach, cold tears streaking her fat cheeks, fear in her eyes. Filina had been digging for clams, hoping to bring a basket back to the cave, where the people had just begun to build their settlement in earnest. She had been shocked at the sight of the child alone—children were precious, the hope for a future, and they were carefully watched over by all.

At first she thought the child must have been one of theirs, but when she approached her she didn't recognize her. She knelt before her and wrapped her in the shawl she'd been wearing, cooing soft words to comfort her. The child was freezing and clung to her tightly.

Then she saw him. A man, huddled by a clump of sea grass, watching. She lifted the child up, glared at the man. A stray, for certain. Some of the people who had survived the bombs had split from the main group—it happened so long ago that Filina didn't even know why. She only knew those people were avoided, and they avoided her people, too. They were rarely seen, and it was thought that most were long dead.

"You should take better care." Filina walked toward the man, ready to hand the child over.

He stood and backed away, shaking his head. "She can't come back." The man held his hands in front of him, warding them both away. "They'll kill her for what she's done."

Filina didn't understand what she was hearing. "What she's done? What can a baby like this do, to deserve to be killed? What sort of barbarians are you people?"

The man stared at the child in Filina's arms. "I'm her father." He met Filina's glare with his own.

"They'll kill her if I bring her back."

"Why?"

The man looked at the sea. He watched the waves rolling in, oblivious to the harsh wind. "She erased her. Her mother." He spoke the words as though he was a robot. "She made her . . . forget." His face crumpled. "I know she didn't do it on purpose. I know she didn't realize. But they'll kill her if I bring her back." His eyes watered, from the wind, or from something else. "I'll kill her myself." He turned his back on her then, on her and his child. Filina had watched in amazement as he stumbled down the beach, watched until she couldn't see him anymore.

It hadn't been easy to hide her. Filina had enlisted Keith's help—well, perhaps enlisted was too mild a term. She'd had him carve a secret unit, just for the girl, all those years ago. She wasn't certain why, but she'd known that Lethe had to be a secret. Little by little she'd learned what the girl had done to her mother, how she made her 'feel better' by helping her forget 'bad' things. Until she made her forget almost everything.

Filina had trained Lethe in her talent, showing her how to use it carefully. She'd chosen people to bring to the secret unit so the child could practice, making certain Lethe erased their memory of being there at all when the session was done. Nobody really noticed that they'd forgotten the color blue, or the smell of eggs. And once Filina had stumbled upon the fact that the child could restore memories as well as remove them, there hadn't been any obstacle to their practice sessions. Still, Filina was extremely cautious. She hadn't really known why she was doing it. But that day that the government men came, it all became clear to her.

She knew it was meant to be this way. The child had been revealed to her, to Filina, because only *she* would have the strength to save her people. Only she would be able to make the sort of sacrifices she'd had to make.

Lethe snuffled breathily in her sleep.

Filina smiled.

Chapter 16

Sarah watched the door of the unit. The rest of the people she'd invited—both of the other amps in the group and three of the dozers—had arrived. People were drinking and laughing, and she hoped none of them noticed the common denominator of the guests. But Jim, the last of the dozers, hadn't come yet.

It was crowded. Sarah's unit wasn't any bigger than the rest even though her father was the man who had carved them. Keith had always laughed with her about carving a huge, grand palace of a unit for their family—at least until her mother had died. He'd stopped laughing about much when the fever took her, but he had always been a good father, and kind to Sarah. Still, fairness was key in the cave. Everyone watched to be certain things were shared equally, and for the most part, they were. Sarah didn't mind that. She did wish the unit was larger tonight, if only because it would be easier to explain having her gathering here rather than in one of the common areas out in the cave. But having this particular gathering here, where it was private, was crucial.

She smiled at a joke someone made, poured more wine for people, and kept her eyes on the door. If Jim didn't show up, all their plans could be ruined.

"Jim!' One of the others announced his arrival. "Where have you been? Late as usual."

Sarah pasted a smile on her face before she offered Jim a drink. "Thought you might not make it." She strained to sound casual.

Jim didn't smile back. He whispered to Sarah. "I need to talk to you. Later." Then he took the drink and turned his attention to the others in the room.

Her smile didn't falter, but Sarah didn't like what she'd heard. Jim sounded worried. She tried to focus on the story one of the amps was telling about how honing had gone that day—something about amping a fire-starter a little too much—but she found it difficult. Finally, when she was arranging more bread on a tray, Jim approached her.

"Everything going all right with you?' He spoke

the words lightly, as though he was just greeting her, but Sarah knew better.

"What's going on, Jim?"

"Filina asked after you."

Sarah kept arranging slices of bread. "So?"

"So she never does that." Jim leaned toward her. "Is something wrong? Are you okay?" He actually sounded concerned.

"I'm fine." Sarah felt a little guilty for what she was about to do, but Jim's words made her even more certain it had to be done. "She's probably just nervous about Celebration. She always gets that way."

"I hadn't noticed that." Jim watched her pick up the tray. He raised his glass to her. "To another year in peace." He studied Sarah's face carefully.

She nodded. "To another year."

"I can take that for you." Jim reached for the tray. "Looks like they could all use refills."

Sarah looked up sharply. He couldn't know, could he? But his face betrayed nothing. He was just offering to help. "Yes, thanks. I'll get the wine." She waited until he was on his way to the table with the bread. Looking around to ensure nobody saw, she slipped a vial out of her pocket and poured it's contents into the wine flask. She gave the flask a quick shake and returned to the table. "Here we go." Sarah smiled gaily. "I heard replenishments were needed." And she poured wine for everyone.

Everyone except herself.

Less than an hour later, Tom tapped quietly at

the door and slipped inside. He surveyed the room, taking in the bodies laid carefully on the floor, tied at wrists and ankles, gags in each mouth. Sarah looked up from where she was finishing the last knot on Jim's wrists.

"I think these will hold." Sarah tugged at the ends of the twine. Then she stood, took a glass from the table. "This one's mine. You know what to do?"

Tom nodded. "I hope this works."

Sarah swallowed the wine. "It has to work." She sat down on the floor next to Jim. "Make it tight." She handed the last of the twine to Tom. "And don't forget the gag."

Chapter 17

It had been a long night. Polly had wakened twice, crying for Hannah. Annie had gone to her each time and tried to comfort her, telling her they would see Hannah soon. Leon slept through it all.

Annie knew his sleeping didn't mean he didn't care. She knew he was as worried about their daughter as she was. As she should have been all this time. To think she'd believed being named Honoree was a great tribute. Leon had known better. He'd wanted to stop her from going, wanted to kill someone, he'd said later. But there was nothing anyone could do. Hannah had gone willingly. At least, it had seemed that way.

Tom had sat the two of them down later and shared his fears. He'd hinted that something was planned, something that might make a difference for the whole community, might even save Hannah. But he'd refused to tell them what. He said it was too dangerous—that if they knew it could put them at risk. Leon had insisted on going right then to the office, to get Hannah back. Annie had gone with him, of course, but they'd been turned away like beggars at a bank entrance.

Now, they would finally see her. Family and friends always did, the morning of Celebration. Filina and her cronies couldn't stop them this time, like they had yesterday. Annie tried not to think about the fact that this might be the *last* time they saw Hannah. She busied herself with breakfast, hoping that Leon was having an easy time getting Polly ready to go.

They hurried through the eggs she'd made, the three of them uncharacteristically somber. Polly just picked at her food, and Annie couldn't blame her.

"Will Hannah come home with us?" Polly's eyes were puffy from her troubled night.

Annie and Leon exchanged a look.

"We'll just have to see, Polly."

It was still early morning, and though the platform and the assembly area were ready for Celebration, few people were around. Annie stared at the platform as they passed it on their way to the office. Celebration had seemed festive to her before, with decorations and mementos symbolizing the year's Honoree, funny stories about them, plenty of food and drink. There were no lessons for the children during Celebration, and the adults ceased their daily labor, too. She'd always been aware of the sadness of the Honoree's family, but she'd pushed that to the back of her mind before. She cringed when she remembered how she'd congratulated Sarah last year about her father, Keith.

Tom waited for them outside the office. Annie thought he looked even worse than he had the day before. She'd told him to come stay with them in their unit, but he'd wanted to stay in his and Hannah's. "Her things are all still there," he'd said.

None of them spoke. Tom waited until they got close and then he turned and knocked on the door. For the longest moment Annie thought it might not open, but finally it did. David held it wide, beckoning them inside.

"She's ready to see you." David started to say more, but Tom brushed past him, none too gently.

Annie, Leon, and Polly followed. Inside, the long table where important meetings were held was lined with empty chairs. At the far end, Hannah sat, looking calm and beautiful. Her hair had been carefully braided and she was wearing a new shirt. Annie couldn't see if she had new pants as well, but she imagined she did. She wondered what had happened to Hannah's other clothes.

"Hannah." Tom rushed to her side. He knelt next to her and took her hand in his. "Are you all right?"

Hannah looked at Tom, a slight smile on her

face. She looked down then, at her hand in his, and gently removed it, placing it on her lap. "I'm . . . fine, thank you."

Tom stared into her face. Tears streamed down his cheeks. "I knew it."

Annie hurried to Hannah's other side. She was whispering something—it sounded like a prayer of some sort. She looked at her daughter, but the eyes that returned her gaze were blank. "What's going on here?" Annie turned on David, who had followed the family to Hannah's side. "What have you done to her?"

David stood looking down at her, implacable. "It's fine, Annie." He shook his head at her as though she were being unreasonable. "They always get a little something to make this part easier. She's just sedated."

"We're taking her home." Leon's voice was low, but he had a look on his face Annie had never seen before. He pushed past David toward where Hannah was sitting.

"Leon." Something in the way David said his name made Leon turn. "You aren't taking her anywhere. She's the Honoree. And they," David point toward the front of the office, where several men—men Leon knew, had known all his life—had appeared, "will make sure of it."

Leon shook his head. "Ed." He addressed the closest of the men. "Ed, you know me. You know my family. We've worked together to make this place what it is today. Help me get my daughter home."

Ed shifted his weight from one foot to the

other, not meeting Leon's gaze at first. When he finally did look at him, he could only shrug. "You know how this works, Leon. According to him," Ed nodded toward David, "if we don't do this they'll come for us all."

Leon stared past him at the others. They all looked uncomfortable, maybe even ashamed, but none of them volunteered to help. He turned his back on them and spoke quietly to Tom. "We can take them, maybe. We can get Hannah home."

But Tom remained slumped at Hannah's side. "She's not even Hannah, anymore." He choked the words out past his tears. "You don't understand—"

"Is that your doll?" Hannah seemed oblivious to what was happening in the room. She was talking to Polly, who had crept near and was holding her driftwood doll up to her sister.

"Yes." Polly gravely handed it to Hannah. "I want you to keep her."

Hannah took the doll, admiring the carving on the face. She handed it back to Polly. "It's beautiful. But I can't take your doll, little girl." She tilted her head at Polly. "What's your name?"

Annie began to sob.

"Listen." David stepped closer to Leon. "Just enjoy this time. Don't cause any trouble. You only have a few hours before we move her."

Leon raised a fist, stopping it just short of David's jaw. Shaking, he forced his arm back to his side. His face ashen, he slid a chair out from the table and sat down close to Hannah. Annie reached for him, and he took her hands in his.

David watched for a moment, then backed away. As he passed the other men on his way out of the room, he avoided their eyes. He was certain they avoided his, too.

"Everyone ready for this?" Daniel surveyed the group. They'd all gathered outside the units to go to Celebration. Even Nipper seemed on edge. "Do you all have the pads where you can reach them easily?" Each person nodded.

"I think we're ready as we'll ever be." Malgam eyed Rachel. "Are *you* ready?"

Rachel shrugged. She could see the crowd already gathered in front of the platform off in the middle of the cavern. "Let's go before I lose my nerve."

"You don't have to do this, Rachel." Vivian put a hand on Rachel's shoulder. "We can think of some other plan."

Rachel smiled at her. "No, we can't. Besides, this will work." She tried hard to look like she believed it.

"Remember, don't do anything until Filina's said something incriminating," Nandy cautioned. "Otherwise it's our word against hers. She's got too much power for us to win that battle."

They started toward the platform. Pathik hung back with Rachel, letting the others walk ahead of them.

"She's right, you know." He gave Rachel a sidelong look.

"Who?"

"Your mother. You don't have to do this." Pathik lowered his voice. "Especially the part they don't know about."

Rachel kept walking, but she held out her hand to him. After a moment, he shook his head and took it. They walked behind the others to where the crowd was gathered in silence.

"Look at that." Nandy sounded disturbed. She pointed at the platform, which had been decorated with hand-woven ribbon. There were what looked like stations of some sort set up in front of it. At each station, a person sat on a stool, talking. As they neared the first one, Rachel recognized the girl she'd seen sharpening knives, the one Hannah had waved at and called dramatic. The girl was speaking to a few people who stood in front of her station, telling a story. As they drew closer, Rachel realized it was a story about Hannah.

"—and she was always trying to get out of gathering clams." The girl smiled, remembering something fondly. "She would make Tom do all the work and she would just look for sea glass." Her audience chuckled, nodding to each other knowingly.

"Look at *that*." Pathik nodded toward the platform. On it, to one side, was a sketch of Hannah. It was a good likeness, done with charcoal on the back of an old board, held aloft in a makeshift easel lashed together with twine. A bowl filled with sea glass sat beneath it.

"Creepy." Malgam frowned. "Like a funeral of some sort."

"More like a fair of some sort, in other ways." Nandy watched as a small group of children ran through the crowd, playing tag. "Lots of food, lots of socializing going on."

"Here we go." Daniel stopped walking. The others stopped, too and looked in the direction he indicated. Filina was making her way across the platform to where the sketch of Hannah was, watching the crowd as she walked. She moved slowly, with a stately manner. When she'd reached the sketch, she stood next to it, waiting for the crowd to quiet.

It didn't take long. Once all was silent, Filina put a hand on the top of the board, inspecting the sketch with interest.

"A wonderful rendering of our Honoree." Filina spoke with pride. "Let us thank Ronnel, the artist responsible for this year's portrait. It will hang with pride of place in Hannah's parents' home." She waited for the applause from the crowd to dwindle. "Please enjoy the refreshments prepared for you all, and thank those who labored over them. And do stop to hear Hannah's remembrances, told by her friends and loved ones." Filina paused, her expression growing serious. "Let us never forget the sacrifice our Honorees make. They willingly give so much in order that we may be spared. Let us always—"

"Willingly?" Rachel shouted the question at the top of her lungs. Daniel, Malgam, and Pathik moved to form a protective wall behind her, while Vivian and Nandy stood in front of her.

Filina glared down at her. The crowd began to murmur, low waves of sound passing from one group to another.

"They don't go *willingly*, do they, Filina?" Rachel shouted again.

Filina strode to the edge of the platform and stared. Rachel could feel it—the spidery touch of Filina's mind, trying to gain entry, trying to control her. She fought to focus, pushing it away. She turned toward the crowd. "You've all been told a lie! You've been told lies for years!"

The noise from the crowd increased. People began to talk—Rachel could hear snippets of questions, comments. *What does she mean? You know, I heard—. That's what Tom said!* As soon as she let her focus go to them, she felt Filina's touch again, a fog, lurking at the edge of her consciousness. She fought it off hard, staring back up at Filina. She could tell she was winning by the look of frustration on her face.

Suddenly, the fog vanished. Rachel saw Filina search the crowd, seeking a certain face. "She's looking for Sarah!" Nandy shouted to Rachel, warning her.

Rachel watched as Filina failed to locate Sarah, who could amp her talent and allow her to overcome Rachel's resistance. Sarah had said she would do this. She'd said Filina would seek all the amps, all the dozers. That's why she wasn't here to help, why she'd made certain none of them were here. If all had gone as planned, they were slumbering, drugged beyond Filina's reach.

Rachel watched fury streak across Filina's face as she realized she couldn't find them. But there was no time for jubilance yet. She turned back to the crowd and shouted.

"Listen! Listen to me! Filina's controlling you all! She's made you believe what she wants you to believe! None of the Honorees went willingly! We know the government! You do too, don't you? The same government that left your people here to die?" She watched their faces, watched them show their fear, their disbelief, their shock. But Filina wasn't admitting anything. Rachel turned to face her. "Tell them Filina. Tell them the truth. Tell them why their Honorees go. And better yet, tell them why they never come back!"

"Why *don't* any of them ever come back?" A voice in the crowd shouted the question. "It's supposed to be a year. A *one* year study. But none of them ever come back."

"My Melissa didn't want to go! I know she didn't!" A woman sobbed the words.

Rachel watched Filina. She could feel her attempts to control her, but it seemed easier each time to resist. Filina was enraged, her skin mottled white and red, her mouth a grimacing slash in her face. She screamed, a shriek that sprayed spittle on Rachel and silenced the crowd. "Where's Sarah? Where are the rest?"

"They won't be helping you today." Rachel spat the words at the woman. Then she smiled up at her.

That was what it took. "Do you think I need *them* to shut you up?" Filina sneered at Rachel.

"Who are you people to come here and judge me? I've saved this place! I've made it possible for us to keep on living!" She narrowed her eyes. "Anyone with a knife can be made to stop the likes of you!" She turned her glare on Daniel.

He shouted a warning, realizing it was him she wanted, feeling her slip into his mind. But they had come prepared. Vivian wrapped her arms around Daniel, covering his mouth with a cloth pad. Almost instantly he slumped and she cradled him to the ground.

"We aren't that stupid, Filina." Malgam shouted up at her, then turned to the crowd. "She's trying to control whoever she can now, to stop Rachel from telling you the tru—" Malgam's words cut off abruptly. He stiffened and reached for his knife. Nandy tried to grab him, but he shook her off easily. Pathik leapt on his back to avoid his knife and was spun around briefly before he could slap his pad on Malgam's mouth. Soon enough though, Malgam tumbled to the ground, unconscious, taking Pathik with him.

"Enough of this." Nandy signaled Nipper. He crouched low, then leapt to the platform and was upon Filina in a moment. She screamed and scratched at him, but she couldn't stop him. He had her down instantly, his mouth covering her throat. Nandy leapt up after him and plastered her drug-soaked pad over Filina's nose. When she went limp, Nipper grudgingly released her throat, tail lashing.

Rachel stood her ground in front of the platform. "Filina isn't hurt." She watched the crowd warily. "Just drugged, so she can't try to control anyone." People were whispering, and some of them had drawn weapons. She waited, every nerve taut, to see what they would do. Finally, one man spoke. "How do we know what you're saying is the truth?"

Rachel knew there was nothing she could say to reassure them. She took a breath, watched as two men advanced, blades drawn.

"Why don't you come see Hannah?" It was Tom. He strode through the crowd to the foot of the platform. His eyes were bloodshot, his face twisted with pain. "Come see what's left of Hannah. *That* should show you what's true and what's not."

Chapter 18

She doesn't even know me." Tom sat next to Sarah on the floor of her unit, untying the last of the twine that had bound her wrists. He'd given her the antidote to the drug she and the others had drunk the night before. She was still groggy, but the effects were fading fast. She was just relieved to be alive. Though she hadn't told Tom, she'd been uncertain whether the antidote would actually work. The woman who'd provided both drugs—one of the strays—hadn't inspired great confidence. It was a chance Sarah felt she'd had to take.

"I have to get to the office." Sarah rubbed her

wrists. "Can you take care of them?" She nodded toward the others, still drugged.

Tom just stared dully at the twine in his hands.

"I'm sorry." Sarah knelt next to him. "Tom, I'm so sorry we couldn't save Hannah. But right now we have to keep going, we have to try to change things." She put a hand on his shoulder. "She's still here, Tom. She's still alive, at least."

He nodded. "I'll see to them." He looked around at the people lying on the floor. They were people he'd known all his life. People who had become potential threats, all because of Filina. "Can you check on her, when you get there?"

"I will." Sarah stood. "Listen, Tom. Wake Jim up first. Don't untie him until you've had a chance to explain. Tell him I'm sorry. Tell him . . ."

"You go." Tom started untying Jim's ankles. "I'll be there as soon as I can."

People crowded into the office. They all had questions. Leon tried to answer as many as he could, but everyone kept talking at the same time. Finally, Daniel climbed onto the table and put his fingers between his lips, whistling shrilly. Relative silence fell, and everyone looked up at him.

"Listen. Listen, all of you. I know this is all very shocking and confusing. But we need to try to stay calm. When Hannah doesn't show up wherever she was supposed to for transport the government will come looking. We need to have a plan."

"Got him!" Two men came in holding David between them. He struggled half-heartedly, knowing he wouldn't escape. "He was in his unit packing up."

Hannah's mother had alerted them that David was gone as soon as they arrived at the office. He'd run when he'd heard the commotion outside. Daniel and Malgam both thought he might have some answers, so they'd asked for volunteers to go find him.

Leon started toward David, his intent evident in his raised fist.

"Hold up." Malgam stepped in front of Leon. "We need him talking, at least right now."

Leon nodded, but he leaned toward David. "Later, my friend, you'll get yours."

"Is it true none of them really wanted to stay? Is that true?" A woman screamed at David from the back of the room. "Where's my girl, if she didn't decide to stay on the mainland? Where is she?"

David stared at the floor.

"Answer her!" someone else yelled.

"Stop." Sarah pushed her way through the crush of people to stand in front of David. She looked at him, contempt curling her lip. "What we need to know is how many usually come, David. How many come to pick up the Honoree? Where do they meet? Do we have any chance of fighting them?"

"She's right." Daniel hopped down from the table. "Is he the one who usually takes them?"

Sarah nodded. "I think so. Filina is always on the platform at Celebration and it's sometime during that they leave to go to the pick-up point, I think."

"You act like you haven't helped her." David

spoke so the whole room could hear. "Like you're blameless in all of this."

Sarah looked like she might break down just then. "I'm not innocent. But I never helped her without being forced to—unlike you."

"She saved us." David straightened, looked around the room. "She was the one person who had the courage to do what needed to be done—she saved all of you. Who here wants to die? That's what they'll do to us, if we don't cooperate and give them what they want."

"They want lab rats, you fool." Malgam spat at David's feet. "They want to see if they can find a way to use your gifts in their wars. They want subjects to experiment on, to test. And if they find a way, they'll use all of you." Malgam turned to the crowd. "He's right about one thing, though. You *all* have a part in this. Trading your Honorees—your own people—for another year of your own lives. Filina can't control all of you, all the time. You've told yourselves the story you want to believe."

People shuffled and mumbled. Tension rose in the room, like an animal rising from a crouch. Sarah, who had listened to Malgam's pronouncements with tears streaming down her cheeks, spoke.

"You're probably right. We're all guilty." She looked around at the people in the room. "Some of us more than others. But we'll have to deal with that later. Right now, we need to know where they're coming to get Hannah." She turned back to David. "How many will come? How can we fight them?"

David shook his head. "Filina won't like this.

You can't keep her drugged forever."

"Filina doesn't run things anymore. Just—"

"We can't fight them and win." It was Rachel, her voice strong. "Not this way." She walked to the table, stepped up onto it like her father had before her. She surveyed the crowd, her gaze stopping at the woman who had screamed out about her daughter, then at Sarah, then Malgam. Finally, she found Pathik and looked into his blue eyes while she spoke. "They have the power, but they have it because of fear. We can't win as long as fear controls us."

"But we *are* afraid."

Rachel couldn't tell who spoke the words. She knew it didn't really matter. "Maybe," she said, "*they're* the ones who should be afraid."

Chapter 19

It was all arranged. David had finally revealed the place—on the far beach in one of the old shacks—where the Honorees were picked up each year. "They have a small crew on the boat, but they only send one to the pick-up point. The rest stay on the boat waiting." His expression made it clear he thought the whole plan was a grave mistake.

Instead of Hannah, Rachel would go, escorted by Jim, who had shown up at the office shortly after Sarah. He'd listened to Rachel's idea and agreed that it could work. He knew the location of the shack and he knew in theory how the pick-up went, so he seemed to be the best choice to take her. He appeared to be eager to help, and very much shaken to learn how much he'd been controlled by Filina.

"I guess I can't blame you for drugging me," he'd said to Sarah. "Or any of us, for that matter. She would have used us to get what she wanted today, just like she's done all along."

Vivian had been a harder sell. "You can't be serious." She'd shaken her head in that way mothers shake their heads when they are not going to change their minds. "No. Absolutely not."

Rachel didn't budge. "It has to be me. I'm about her age, and that's what they expect this year."

"There are plenty of other girls around her age in their own group—"

"This is *our* group now, Mother." Rachel sounded angry. "We came here looking for a place to start a better life. *This* is the place. *These* are the people. We have to start somewhere."

Vivian studied her daughter's face. She sighed. "I'm being a coward again, aren't I, Rachel?" She whispered the words.

Rachel frowned. She knew how much that accusation—made at a time when she had understood so much less about loss—had hurt her mother. "You're not a coward. You just want to protect the people you love. But you know I'm right. I already know how to use a stunner—none of them do. If I can get his stunner, we've got a chance.

Vivian nodded, but she still looked troubled. "Well, we've got a hostage. One the rest of the government would probably let die with no qualms at all. Where does that get us?"

"As soon as he sees the copy of the map, he'll know we mean business. We'll have him scan it and send it to his commander and they'll *have* to leave us alone."

Vivian looked doubtful, but Daniel, who had been listening quietly, spoke up.

"I think it could actually work. The maps are probably still pretty accurate and they show every weak spot there is in the Border Defense System. Given the nature of the technology the systems run on, those weaknesses can't be helped—they'll always be vulnerable. Once the Unified States knows we have a map revealing theirs, and that we can release it to Unifolle, or worse, to Korusal, they'll want to work with us. Then it's just a matter of letting Unifolle and Korusal know we have theirs, too, and we're untouchable."

"So much could go wrong," said Vivian. She sighed. "But I know we have no other choice." She held out her hands to her daughter and her husband. The three of them sat together, silently holding hands, for as long as they could.

Too soon, Jim interrupted them. "We have to go in a few minutes. You sure you're ready for this?"

Rachel nodded. "I have to do something first." She hugged Vivian and Daniel, then walked toward the smaller room off the office, where she knew Tom sat with Hannah.

The room was quiet, unlike the office itself, which was still buzzing with people. Leon and

Annie had insisted that Tom and Hannah be given some space. They'd stood guard at the door to the little room, letting Tom take what solace he could in Hannah's physical presence. Annie made an exception for Rachel when she whispered in her ear, explaining her visit.

Rachel felt like she was interrupting a funeral when she walked into the room. "Tom," she whispered.

Tom and Hannah both looked up. Tom's eyes held recognition; Hannah offered only the polite gaze most people reserved for pleasant strangers.

"Rachel." Tom smiled, though it was clear to Rachel it was a façade, empty of feeling, forged for Hannah's benefit.

"I have to go soon, but I wanted to give you something." Rachel dug in her pocket. "Han—um, it was given to me for safekeeping. In case I needed to get it to you." She fished out the fabric packet Hannah had trusted her with and handed it to Tom. She leaned down and whispered in his ear. "She loved you so much."

Tom took the packet, turning it in his hands. Hannah looked at it, but gave no sign that she knew what it was.

"Is it . . ." Tom let his words die unspoken. He knew what it was, knew Hannah would have thought of everything. He knew he would spend many hours reading and rereading whatever words she'd left him. "Thank you."

Rachel put a hand on his shoulder. "I'll see you later." She smiled at Hannah, who seemed bemused.

"Take care of yourself, Hannah."

Pathik stood waiting, right outside the doorway. He met her eyes, his own as serious as she'd ever seen them.

"Are you sure?"

Rachel stood before him, trying to find the right words to reassure him, but finally, all she could do was nod. "I'd better get going."

"Scared?" Pathik didn't move out of her way.

She shrugged. "Not too much."

"You know I know better."

Rachel grinned. "Where's all that Usage training? You're not supposed to sniff around reading my feelings without my permission."

Pathik grinned, too. "I'm not using my gift. I just know you." He stepped closer, drew her near and there, in front of all the people in the office, he kissed her. It was a long, soft kiss, one that Rachel wished could never end. When he finally let her go, he looked shyly at her. "I'd like to keep on knowing you, so be careful."

"It's still a ways off." Jim tried to sound confident, but Rachel could tell he was as nervous as she was. They'd been walking for a long time. Just getting down the mountainside had taken hours. The trail was narrow and treacherous. At one point, when they negotiated a particularly nasty switch-back, Rachel looked slyly at Jim. "You had to carry me up this, huh?"

Jim looked uncomfortable, remembering his part in abducting her. "Um. Sorry about that."

"You should be." Rachel didn't say any more about it.

They'd set off alone, without announcing their departure to anyone but Rachel's group. At first, they hadn't been sure how they'd manage to slip out—the office had still been buzzing with people, everyone asking questions, nobody having any real answers. Sarah had finally gone out to the platform to address everyone in the cave, to try to explain what was happening. Rachel and Jim had taken advantage of the crowd's diverted attention to take their leave.

When they finally touched the beach, Rachel was too tired to feel nervous. "How far now?"

Jim looked down the beach, eyeing the tide. "It's just past that little cove. We'll be there before you know it."

They trudged on. Neither of them saw the furtive figure behind them, darting from the cover of a dune to a clump of sea grass.

"I am sorry, you know." Jim spoke so quietly that Rachel had to strain to hear him over the sound of the waves.

She looked up at him and saw he was crying. He swiped at the tears on his cheek almost angrily.

"I didn't know. I didn't know about Filina, how she was controlling me."

"She controlled a lot of people." Rachel stepped over a waxy kelp bulb. "I just wish we could make her undo what she did to Hannah. At least then *one* family wouldn't have lost so much."

"What do you mean?"

"Wiping her—making her forget everyone, even Tom." Rachel thought of the slim fabric packet, all that was left of Hannah's love for Tom.

"Filina didn't do that. It was Lethe."

"Who's Lethe?"

Jim stopped walking. "Wait a minute." He bit his lower lip as though it helped him think. His expression went from thoughtful to excited. "Lethe! Filina said she could take them away and bring them back."

"What are you talking about?" Rachel wondered if he'd gone mad.

Jim took hold of her shoulders. "Lethe is a little girl—a stray I think. She's the one who takes their memories. Filina's kept her a secret for years. Filina said *she can take, but she can give back, too*. I think maybe she can reverse what she's done to Hannah."

Rachel stared. "Do you know where she is now?"

Jim nodded. "As soon as we get back I'll get her. She's locked in her unit—Filina made sure of that."

"You're late."

The voice startled both of them. Jim instinctively reached for his knife, but stayed his hand at the sight of the stunner pointed at him. The man who held it shook his head.

"I wouldn't." He waved the stunner, directing them to move ahead of him. "What took you so long?"

Jim replaced his knife in its sheath. "We got a late start this time."

The man spoke into a comm unit clipped on his shoulder. "On our way." He stepped closer and gripped Rachel's arm. "I can take it from here."

Jim stood, looking uncertain. "We usually meet in the shack."

"Well, you were late. Made me come out here in the wind to find you." The man made a shooing gesture. "Go on, now. I said I can take it from here."

Rachel hadn't taken her eyes off the stunner. She rammed her body hard into the man's side, knocking him off balance. As he fell, she grabbed for the stunner but it flew from her hands, landing in the sand a few feet away.

"Get it!" Jim threw himself on the man, trying to hold him down. Rachel scuttled over the sand, almost there, reaching, but a hand slammed down on top of hers just as she grasped the stunner. The man pried her fingers off and rolled, pointing it at Jim. Rachel watched him fall. She tried to scramble away, but the man kicked her feet out from under her. She landed on her back in the sand.

The last thing she saw was the stunner, as the man raised it and pointed it at her face.

Chapter 20

"She's fine, lucky for you."

Rachel woke to the sight of two men in uniforms, one snapping a scanner back into its case. The other she recognized as the man on the beach. She was lying on a metal cot that was attached to the wall. She tried to sit up, but her wrist was shackled to one of the cot brackets.

"Settle down." The man with the scanner case frowned at her. "You've caused enough trouble. Just relax and enjoy the ride."

"The ride?" Rachel became aware then, of a humming sound. There was a jolt, and the humming sound grew louder.

"Full speed ahead." The man from the beach looked at the ceiling. "I'll go above, see what they want to do about the whole thing. They were still waiting on a return comm when I came down."

"They won't do much. They still want a steady supply of these, from what I hear. If they blow the whole bunch up, who will they run their experiments on?"

"You're probably right." The man from the beach ducked through a hatch and disappeared. Rachel could see his legs and then his feet as he climbed a ladder just outside the hatch.

They were in a boat. And they were moving. Rachel felt a wave of panic rush through her body. She tried to slow her breathing—she needed to think.

The map. It was in her jacket pocket—but her jacket was gone. She reached for her pocket but her jacket was gone. "Where's my coat?"

The man who remained shrugged. "Who knows? You won't need it where you're going."

"You have to find my coat!" Rachel struggled to sit up again.

The man raised his hand above her head, holding it there as though he couldn't decide whether to hit her or not. "Listen, quiet down." He frowned and lowered his hand. "You're not in a position to be making demands. They'll get you all the clothes you need when we get there." He smirked. "All of them will probably tie in back and flap in the wind, too."

A siren began to wail. At the same time, a red light set into the wall near the hatch lit up. "What now?" The man went to the opposite wall and pushed a button. He spoke into a mesh square that reminded Rachel of Ms. Moore's front door intercom. "Gordon here. Should I report?"

A tinny voice came from the mesh. "One of them stowed away!"

"What? What did you say?"

"One of them stowed away and he got a stunner. Almost blasted Ramsey before they got him. They're bringing him your way, so pop another cot. Received?"

Gordon turned to look at Rachel. He twisted back to speak into the mesh, never taking his eyes off of her. "Received. Over." He let go of the button on the wall and stepped closer. "What's this, then? One of your friends didn't want to say good bye?"

Rachel shook her head. "I don't know what you're talking about. I need my coat."

"Sure you do." Gordon turned his back on her, bending down to unlatch a cot on the opposite wall.

There was noise in the hall, and someone banged on the ladder. A disembodied voice called out. "Gordo! Come help me with this guy."

Gordon stepped out and Rachel could see him reach up toward the ladder. He wrapped his arms around something and began to back into the room.

"Wait—watch his head." The voice was closer.

Rachel saw what Gordon had hold of—the lower half of someone's body. She watched as it dropped from above, then jerked to a stop as the man who had called for help grabbed an arm.

"Almost dropped him, you fool!" Gordon staggered a bit and adjusted his hold. He lifted the legs higher as the other man reached the bottom of the ladder still clinging to the body's arm. The two hauled the person into the room and plopped him onto the cot Gordon had readied.

Rachel could only stare.

It was Pathik.

His face was bloody. Rachel could see a rip in his pants. His arms flopped limply when the men put him on the cot. Gordon immediately wrapped a cuff like the one Rachel had around Pathik's wrist and snapped it onto the cot bracket.

"Got it from here?" The other man wiped his forehead with the back of his hand. He was breathing heavily.

"Yep." Gordon smirked at the man. "You ought to do more push-ups, don't you think?"

"Shut up." The man didn't smile. "They said to check the head wound. He got hit pretty hard."

Gordon nodded. "Will do.

The other man ducked back out through the hatch and Rachel listened to the clanging sound his feet made as he ascended the ladder. Gordon unsnapped the scanner case and ran the device over Pathik's forehead. He pushed Pathik's hair away and winced at the wound. "Bet that hurt." He re-cased the scanner and popped open a bin, rummaging for something. Withdrawing a flat packet, he ripped open the top of it and removed a moistened pad.

Rachel smelled a stringent scent. "Is he all right?"

Gordon twisted his neck to look back at her. "He's fine. Nothing a little alcohol swab won't fix." He scrubbed at Pathik's forehead, removing most of the blood. "He'll be sleeping a while, though."

Rachel couldn't stop the tears welling up in her eyes. "I need you to find my coat."

Gordon raised his eyes to the ceiling and made a sound. "And I need you to shut up." He shook his head. "Your boyfriend here is nice and quiet. And I think it's time for *you* to go nighty-night, so Gordo here doesn't have to listen to your blather all the way back to port." He popped open another bin and took a small, preloaded hypodermic needle out. Stepping over to Rachel, he uncapped the needle and without a word, he stuck it in her upper arm. She jumped at the pain, then realized what he had done.

"No! No. I need you to find my coat, I need—" Rachel's head lolled to the side.

"There we go." Gordon tossed the needle and the alcohol pad into a trash receptacle. "That's better."

She awoke in a small room. She lay on another cot. There was a toilet. That seemed to be all. The front of the room was glass, with wire embedded in it in a crisscross pattern. The back and sides were cement. There was a door in one of the sides. She didn't have to check to know that it was locked. She looked down and saw that she was dressed in a jumpsuit, made from some thin, plastic-feeling fabric.

She could see a duplicate of the room she was in across from her, beyond the glass wall and a hallway. Someone lay on the cot there, wearing the same sort of jumpsuit she had on. The person wasn't moving. Her eyes didn't seem to want to focus enough for her to tell if the person was Pathik.

She listened. There was nothing to hear. When her vision had cleared more, she sat up, relieved to find that she wasn't shackled to anything.

She felt so afraid.

What if this was it? What if she never saw Pathik again, or her mother and father? Her thoughts raced, and she shivered, though it wasn't cold in the room. She tried to remember what her father had said about his time as a prisoner in the Roberts camp. About how he'd been sure he was going to die, about how he thought of her and her mother all the time. It made him brave, he said.

Rachel didn't feel very brave.

The figure on the cot across from her stirred. Rachel stood and went to the glass, pressing her hands against it. "Hey." She spoke softly. "Hey, are you awake?"

It wasn't Pathik. It was a woman, her hair bedraggled, her face worn. She looked dully over at Rachel. Slowly, she sat up, but she didn't get off the cot. "You the new one?" She squinted. "Who are you? I don't recognize you."

"I'm Rachel. Who are you?"

The woman shrugged. "You must have been little when they took me." She rose slowly, and walked to her own glass wall. "I'm Melissa." She tilted her head at Rachel. "Did you ever hear about me? Is any of my family still . . . there? Wherever *there* is." The woman frowned. "Still, I don't remember a Rachel. And you're old enough you would have been . . . what? Eleven? Twelve years old when I was still there?"

"You're the first one they took, right?" Rachel remembered Tom telling the story about Melissa on the beach, about the men coming from nowhere. About Filina, handing her over. "How do you remember?"

"What do you mean?"

"I thought Filina took you to Lethe before she handed you over." Rachel waited, but Melissa didn't say anything. "Lethe, the one who makes them all forget."

Melissa nodded, then. "The little girl, right? She took me to her. I didn't understand what was happening." She looked up and down the hallway. "The others don't remember anyone at all. I think the little girl wasn't as good with her talent back then, when she did me."

Rachel looked down the hall, too. Are they here? The others?"

Melissa nodded. "You can't see from your cell, but there's a whole row. When they take you to the labs, you walk by." She bowed her head. "That's the only time I see them."

There was a sound far down the hall—the sound of a door opening. Melissa shrank back from the glass. She ran to her cot and lay down, turning her face to the wall. Rachel felt her heart beating fast. She could hear footsteps echoing down the hall, coming closer and closer. She wanted to run back to her cot, too, but she forced herself to stand, calmly, at the glass.

Chapter 21

Malgam burst through the unit door. Nandy had brought Nipper here to get him away from the people in the office. They still didn't understand about Nipper; they only saw a huge, wild animal. Many of them had seen him attack Filina on the platform, too. All the sideways looks he was getting had made Nandy nervous. "Pathik's gone." Malgam sounded as close to panicked as Nandy had ever heard him.

"What do you mean, gone?"

"Gone!" Malgam took a breath. "Sorry. I don't mean to yell at you. But he's gone. The boat's gone,

Rachel's gone, and now Pathik." Malgam's jaw muscle jumped. "Jim said he didn't see him following but I bet he was."

"He wouldn't be seen if he didn't want to be." Nandy hesitated. "Do you think . . ." She looked away.

"What?"

Nandy wished she hadn't spoken. "Could you try to see? See if he's . . ."

Malgam nodded, understanding immediately. He could use his gift to try to see what Pathik was seeing. If he was alive, he'd know.

Nandy held his arm. "I'm sorry." Malgam had used his gift like this before, and that time, he'd seen the death of his father, Indigo. He'd never spoken of it since, but Nandy knew it caused him immeasurable pain.

Malgam sat down on a stool. He closed his eyes, concentrating.

"Do you think he could have gotten on the boat?" Nandy was worried.

"Shhh." Malgam gave her a look.

"Sorry."

Once again Malgam closed his eyes. He focused deeply, searching for his son's sight. He was tentative at first, filled with dread at the prospect of seeing only emptiness. Emptiness meant death. Behind his eyelids, shapes swam in and out of focus. They began to form other shapes, until they all came together. Malgam could see cloth, a strange sort of fine cloth. He saw a hand come into focus, resting on the cloth. He knew the hand—would know it anywhere. "He's alive."

Malgam kept his eyes closed, looking for more. Nandy was silent, waiting. He saw his son's hand, and then Pathik must have looked up, because everything swirled for a moment. Then, the shapes coalesced again, forming into what Pathik was looking at—a wall. A wall of glass. Then, it was all gone.

Malgam shook his head. "I didn't get much. But he's alive. In some . . . glass room of some sort."

"I knew it. He got on the boat." Nandy scowled. "He wouldn't have let them take her without following."

Malgam nodded. "He loves her." He looked up at Nandy. "I'd follow you, too."

Nandy looked down at him, smiling. She kissed his lips softly, trying to take some of his anguish away. "We'll get them both back."

They left hand in hand, to tell the others what Malgam had seen.

Daniel and Vivian were talking with Jim. He'd returned alone, bruised and bloodied. When Daniel, who'd been waiting at the cave's entrance, saw his lone figure approaching, he'd fallen to his knees. Jim had expected him to strike out, to blame him for losing Rachel, but Daniel had only looked up, waiting for Jim to tell him what had happened.

Vivian had not been so forgiving. She'd flung herself at Jim, pounding at him, until Daniel wrapped his arms around her and held her tight while she gained control.

"It's nobody's fault," he'd whispered to her, over and over.

"I don't know what happened after he pointed the stunner. When I woke they were gone." Jim looked as anguished as Vivian did.

They tried to come up with a plan. But even with Malgam's assurance that Pathik still lived, the atmosphere in the office was grim.

It was Vivian who turned the tide. She'd been watching Daniel grow more and more subdued, watching as he seemed to lose hope before her eyes. She thought about all the years she'd believed he was dead, about how blessed she was now, to have him back, alive and well. She thought about Rachel, so brave, so eager to make a difference.

"If Pathik's alive, I bet Rachel is, too." She said the words softly, but Daniel heard. He turned to look at her.

"And she's doing what she believes must be done." Vivian squeezed her husband's hand, and stood. "So, first things first."

"What do you mean, first things first?" Daniel sounded tired.

"We have to be ready for what comes." Vivian, ever practical, began to organize. "Who's making meals?" She looked around the room. Everyone will need their strength. "You." Vivian pointed at Tom. You take Hannah and go get some food."

Tom just stared, but Annie, who was listening, jumped up. "Exactly!" She took Hannah's hand. "Come on dear. I know you've forgotten a lot, but I bet you can still make a sandwich."

Hannah nodded, though she looked slightly amazed. "I can make soup, too."

Annie grinned. "Then, off we go!"

Vivian watched them leave and then looked at Sarah. "Who's making sure that Filina stays drugged?"

Sarah nodded. "Every hour on the hour is the dose. I'll see to it."

"And Malgam." Vivian took a deep breath. "I know it's tiring, but how often can you check in on Pathik? I think we should have a schedule, so we can tell if anything is happening."

Malgam eyed her. "I always knew you were bossy." He looked at Nandy. "Will you keep watch over me?" When he was using his gift he was vulnerable, and Malgam trusted few. There were too many strangers in the office for his taste.

"You know I will." Nandy put her arm around him. "With my life."

Malgam nodded. "Keep an eye on that one especially," he joked, pointing at Vivian.

"I can go get the girl. " Jim stood and looked around. "Lethe, I mean. She's locked in that unit alone."

"Bring her here, where we can feed her. It's better if we keep her close until everyone understands what she's done isn't her fault." Vivian lowered her voice so Leon wouldn't hear. "Don't get anyone's hopes up about her, yet."

Jim had shared his theory about Lethe, that she might be able to reverse the memory loss she caused. "I won't."

"What can I do?" Daniel stared up at his wife, marveling at her. He looked less burdened already.

"You can go and get some blankets. I think we'll make this our command station, for the duration. We'll need places to curl up for some sleep." Vivian smiled at Daniel.

She kept smiling, too, until he'd left the office and she had a chance to duck into the little room where Hannah had been kept. Only then did she let her tears fall.

It felt like they would never stop.

Chapter 22

The footsteps came closer, until Rachel could see that they belonged to a man. He was holding a digitab, reading the screen as he walked, its glow lighting his face so that his cheekbones jutted out like a skull's. He didn't look up until he was standing directly in front of Rachel.

"I see you're awake." When he finally did look at her, Rachel knew she was right to be afraid. His eyes were like a spider's eyes: soulless, cold, investigative.

"I need to get my coat back." Rachel was pleased at how firm her voice sounded.

"Yes." The man swiped his finger across the digitab's screen, reading some notation. "They said you kept saying that." He was completely uninterested in her request.

"I need to show you something that's in it—in the pocket." Rachel waited. The man said nothing. He swiped his screen a few more times, then tilted his head toward his shoulder and spoke into the comm unit clipped there. "I'll need lab room three, I think."

"Did you hear me?" Rachel truly wasn't certain whether he had heard her or not.

The man raised his eyes to her again. "I heard you." He looked displeased. "You'll come with me now." He walked toward the door in her cell and touched something on his side of the wall. The door clicked. The man pointed at the door. "Push it open and come with me."

Rachel didn't know what else to do. She went to the door and pushed it. It was heavy. When she'd swung it open enough, she slipped through and into the hallway. She saw that Melissa hadn't turned from the wall in her cell.

"Follow me." The man turned and began to walk away without looking back.

Rachel followed slowly. Melissa had been telling the truth; there were cells all along the hallway. Rachel looked into each one as she passed them. One held another girl, this one sitting up on her cot, staring as Rachel walked by. The next two were empty. Another held a man, who stood as close to the glass of his cell as he could. He watched Rachel walk by, a confused expression on his face.

Rachel slowed her pace even more. She wondered if the man was Keith. "Do you know Sarah?" She tried to whisper, but the man ahead of her heard. He simply smiled though, a smile without any warmth, and waited by the door at the end of the hallway.

"I know Sarah!" Melissa spoke loudly from her cell. "That's Keith you see, her father. Are you seeing him? A man with gray hair and a beard?"

"I see him." Rachel stole a glance at the man waiting at the end of the hall. He seemed bored, but resigned. He was reading his digitab while he waited.

"He doesn't remember Sarah." Melissa sounded sad. "He doesn't remember any of us."

The man with the beard searched Rachel's eyes from his side of the glass wall. He looked like he was a nice man, a kind man. "She's okay," Rachel whispered. "Don't worry, Sarah's okay." She knew he wouldn't understand what she meant, but she felt better saying it even so.

The man at the end of the hall cleared his throat. Rachel moved forward. She saw two more people, a women and a man, and then she saw Pathik. He was standing next to his glass wall, dressed in the same sort of jumpsuit they all had.

"I heard you coming." He couldn't stop smiling. His forehead was bruised and the cut he'd gotten on the boat had been bleeding again, but he looked so beautiful to Rachel.

"You idiot." She slapped the glass where his face was, making him flinch.

"What kind of hello is that?" He raised his eyebrows. "I kind of expected something nicer."

"You followed us, me and Jim." Rachel put her hand up against the glass.

Pathik put his hand up too, and matched hers finger for finger on the glass. "Obviously it's a good thing I did."

"I can't find my coat."

Pathik frowned. "That doesn't seem like our biggest problem right now."

"It has the map in the pocket."

"Oh."

Rachel just nodded.

"Yes. Total recognition."

Pathik and Rachel both heard the man's voice at the same time. Rachel peered down the hall. "He's talking into his shoulder thing."

"Confirmed." The man sighed. "I'll bring them both." He started walking back toward Rachel. When he reached the door to Pathik's cell he touched the place in the wall that unlocked it. "You," he said to Pathik. "Come along. They want to see the two of you together." He slipped one hand into his pocket and withdrew a stunner. "Don't try anything."

"I saw Rachel!" Malgam shouted, startling Nandy, who'd been sitting quietly by his side while he sought Pathik's vision once more. Malgam jumped up and slapped Daniel on the back. He saw Vivian's face and gave her a long hug. "She's fine," he whispered. "She looked good."

Vivian was overcome. "Oh." She wiped her eyes with her sleeve. "Oh, thank you, Malgam."

"Then there's hope." Daniel smiled. "There's still some hope."

Malgam nodded. He knew how helpless Daniel felt; he felt the same way. He trusted his son, though. If there was a way, Pathik would get Rachel out. Malgam knew what his son's love meant. He was the same as his grandfather, Indigo, about love. Malgam realized something, then. Something about what Indigo had been trying to tell him for so many years about love. What Nandy had been trying to show him about it. He ducked his head for a moment, so that no one could see his tears.

Pathik and Rachel held hands as they walked, the man with the stunner following closely. When they reached the end of the hallway, he motioned them away from the door.

"I'll just get that." He punched a code into the keypad next to the door. When it clicked, he held it open and gestured for them to go through. "Well? Move along."

There was another hallway.

"Third door on the right." The man sounded hurried, now.

The third door on the right opened into a large room. There were three chairs around a small round table. In one of the chairs sat another man, this one older than the first. He looked up from his digitab when they entered, and smiled. "Ah. Finally." The man inspected them without getting up. "Have a seat, please." He nodded toward the chairs facing him. "You may leave us now, Jeffrey."

The other man hesitated. "Do you need Security to come?"

The older man sighed. "I said you may leave us. Now."

Jeffrey scuttled out of the room.

Rachel sat down, but Pathik looked around. There was a metal table on one side of the room, with indented channels running down both sides. Pathik looked down at the floor. There was a drain set into it, just at the end of the table.

"I said to sit down," the man snapped.

Pathik looked up. "I heard you." He ambled to the empty chair, settling himself in it at a leisurely pace. Rachel stared at him. He just shrugged.

"Now then. I'm told the two of you retain your memories." The man narrowed his eyes. "Is that true?"

Neither Rachel nor Pathik answered.

The man stared at them. His eyes were just as soulless as Jeffrey's.

"I need to get my coat back. I have—"

"Yes, yes, you keep *saying* that." The man leaned toward Rachel. "But we simply don't care about your coat."

Pathik took Rachel's hand again. He leaned forward as well, staring at the man. "I think you're going to care."

They appraised each other for several seconds. Finally, the man spoke.

"Why would I care?"

Rachel squeezed Pathik's hand. "You're going to care if you have any concern about the Unified States' Border Defense System." She tried not to look toward the metal table. The counter next to it had several cloths laid out on it, with odd-looking shapes underneath them. She'd watched enough streamer shows to know what those shapes were. Scalpels. Drills. Hemostats. She was glad that Pathik had never seen those shows. *You can't be brave without being afraid. You can't be brave without being afraid.* She chanted the words to herself silently.

The man leaned back in his chair. "This is a research facility. What makes you think I have any concern at all with the BDS?"

"Maybe because of the kind of research you seem to be doing here." Pathik touched the cut on his forehead, wincing. "I think you're going to want to get her coat."

"There's something in one of the pockets," Rachel said, as brightly as she could. She smiled at the man.

"What sort of something might that be?" The man didn't seem happy. Rachel imagined that he was picturing all his happy cutting time slipping away.

"It's a map. Of the entire U. S. Border Defense System. With all of the weaknesses highlighted. We've already sent it along to Unifolle. Of course, they probably won't take advantage of it right away, since the U.S. has an awful lot of treaties with them, don't you? Korusal will be next." Rachel hoped she sounded convincing.

She must have. The man stood up and spoke

into an intercom on the wall. "Was there a coat on the transport? Belonging to one of the subjects?"

Jeffrey's voice came back over the speaker. "I took the liberty of checking, Sir, since it kept coming up." He sounded very proud.

"And?" The man in the room did not sound like Jeffrey was going to get a gold star for his efforts.

"There is a jacket here. The transport crew delivered it just minutes ago."

"Bring it." The man clicked the intercom off and sat back down at the table. He Stared at Rachel, then at Pathik. He said nothing. The three of them waited.

Within moments, there was knock at the door.

"Yes." The man at the table didn't look away from them when he spoke. The door opened a crack. Rachel couldn't see who was there.

"Oh, come in, Jeffrey. All the way in, if you please." The man at the table sounded disgusted. The door opened the rest of the way, and Jeffrey stumbled in holding Rachel's coat out like some sort of offering.

"Here it is, Sir." Jeffrey stuttered out the words.

The man snatched the coat, and began to search the pockets. He withdrew a wrinkled sheet of paper and unfolded it. "This is just some . . . child's drawing." He sneered at the copy of the map Rachel had traced.

Pathik leaned over closer so he could see. "It *is* pretty bad."

Rachel ignored him. "You might want to have

that checked out by someone who knows what they're looking at." She tilted her head at the man. "What's your name, anyway?"

"What's my name got to do with anything?" The man regarded her as though she smelled like rotten meat on a hot day.

"I just want to know what to call you. Sir." Rachel hoped she'd gotten all the lines right when she was tracing the map.

"Jeffrey." The man held the drawing out to Jeffrey without looking away from Rachel. "Have it scanned and sent to Division."

Jeffrey took the paper with shaking hands and quickly disappeared.

"Now." The man folded his arms. "We wait." He looked past Rachel to the towels laid out on the counter, smiling in anticipation.

It took all of twenty minutes. There was a crackle from the wall intercom. "Doctor Wilkinson." The man stood up and walked slowly to the intercom. He pressed the button.

"Yes, Jeffrey."

"You may want to come to the main office."

Rachel and Pathik waited in the room while the man went to see whatever there was to see. Pathik held Rachel's hand in his, smiling at her.

"You shouldn't be smiling yet." Rachel was afraid.

"I think it's going to be all right." Pathik leaned over and kissed her. She let him, but as soon as the kiss ended she pushed him away and scowled.

"You shouldn't have followed us."

He shook his head. "I have to admit, I was scared to do it." He looked ashamed. "But how could I let you go alone?"

"You know what Ms. Moore said." Rachel smiled at him. "You can't be brave if you're not afraid."

Pathik thought of his letter—the letter from his grandmother. *Do what needs to be done, whatever that is, to keep your love alive.* "She was a very smart woman."

Doctor Wilkinson returned, looking a bit shaken. He sat down at the table and folded his hands together. He cleared his throat. He took a deep breath and began to speak. "It appears—"

"So, Doctor Wilkinson." Rachel sat up straight in her chair. "We'll need all the hostages you have here on the transport boat with us. We'll need a stock of supplies as well—antibiotics, some vaccines, whatever else you can think of that might come in handy."

The doctor stared at Rachel, anger flooding his eyes. He stiffened his neck. "It's people like you who threaten the fabric of our nation."

Rachel considered him from across the table. She couldn't help wanting to hurt him. He, and people like him, had hurt so many. But she knew it would make no real difference, except to who she was. She liked who she was, so far.

Pathik squeezed Rachel's hand. He leaned as far over the table as he could without getting up and smiled at Doctor Wilkinson. "I think there are a couple more things we'll need from you."

Chapter 23

Jonathan tried to run up the path to the main house, but his knees wouldn't cooperate. By the time he got there, the EOs were already out of their vehicle and on the front porch. "Here now." He gasped for breath. "Haven't you fools bothered her enough?"

The EOs just stared at him. The one closest to him consulted his digitab. "Are you Jonathan—"

The front door swung open. Elizabeth appeared, her face scrunched up tight with anger. "Leave him alone!" She scolded the EOs as though they were errant children.

"It's all right, Elizabeth." Jonathan climbed the stairs to the landing. "I'm sure these fine boys are just checking on our safety, aren't you?" He glared at the EOs.

The one with the digitab scanned his screen. "I've got orders to deliver a message to Elizabeth Moore." He waited to see if anyone would claim the name.

Elizabeth stepped forward. Jonathan started to protest, but she shook her head wearily. "I'm sick of it, Jonathan." She looked at the EO resentfully. "Deliver your stupid message."

The EO read from his digitab, haltingly. "It's time for you and Jonathan to come join us. Please bring some orchids—I think mine died. And remember what you told me about being brave. Love, Rachel." The EO looked up.

Elizabeth frowned. "Let me see that." She grabbed the digitab from the EO. After she read the message, she looked at Jonathan.

He shrugged. "What?"

"I don't know!" Elizabeth shrugged back at him.

The second EO stepped forward. "We have orders to deliver Elizabeth Moore and her hired man to the main port in Ganivar, for transport to the relinquished island of Salishan." The EO paused to see if there would be any reaction. There was not. He continued. "If you choose to accept transport we have been allowed one half hour for you to gather any and all items you wish to bring."

Elizabeth looked at Jonathan. Jonathan looked

back at Elizabeth. They both smiled at the same moment. Elizabeth turned to the EO.

"I think we'll need at least an hour, son."

Fisher tossed one more log onto the camp's central fire. It was early morning and he knew that soon enough people would be seeking its warmth, ready to drink their cups of hot root brew in the company of their fellows.

He'd just returned from his trek the night before.

It had been further then he'd thought it would be—nine days out—to the beach where Indigo had claimed the boats were. Where Pathik and Rachel and their families had journeyed, intent on finding a new start. He didn't know why he'd gone. Perhaps just see the place.

There *were* boats there, just like Indigo had always insisted. Two boats, metal hulls shining in the sun, lacy with rusting bullet holes. He'd felt something fold inside his chest when he saw them. But he looked closer, and he found evidence that' there had been a third. The place where it had rested for who knew how long was clear, and the marks where someone—Pathik? Malgam? Daniel?—had dragged it to the sea were still there. Fisher had smiled, then, and looked out at the ocean.

Maybe they'd made it. He'd thought about it all the way back to camp, wondering if he should have left with them. But there were things that needed to be done here, council meetings to attend, to ensure no one strayed from their good intentions. There was a certain girl who, though she wasn't Rachel, might be enough for him. He sat down on the log bench near the fire and waited for his people to wake, to come talk about the ordinary things they talked about, like who was sick, or who was next up for a hunting trek, or whether the Roberts had been causing trouble of late.

Kinec ran up to the fire, so pale, so out of breath that Fisher thought he must have been chased by a baern at first. He was up with his blade drawn immediately, looking past Kinec for the beast. They rarely ventured so close to camp, but one never knew.

"Fisher!" Kinec gasped for air, his chest heaving. He bent over and put his hands on his knees until he could speak. "A flying machine!"

Fisher crinkled his brow. "A what?"

"A flying machine!" Kinec straightened. "I was checking the traps and it just *appeared* above me. It made no sound at all." Kinec reconsidered. "Well, very little sound. And a man dropped from it on a line, like some sort of fish, or . . . something like that."

Fisher didn't know what to think. He wondered if Kinec was telling the truth. The boy did tend toward exaggeration.

"He waved to me. To me!" Kinec was speaking more calmly now. "And he handed me this." He fished a piece of paper out of his pack. "They must think we're pretty stupid."

Fisher took the paper. He saw what Kinec

meant. There was a section of text, but above that was a sort of picture-message, intended to ensure the communication was understood if the recipients couldn't read. Fisher skipped to the text.

His eyes grew wider and wider as he read.

"Go get Michael." Fisher reread the message twice before he realized that Kinec was still standing there. "Go get Michael, please."

Kinec nodded, but he didn't leave. "Do you think it's true? Would they really leave us boats?"

Fisher could only nod. "I think Rachel must have figured out a way to get the upper hand." He smiled as he read the message a third time. "I don't know who else would come up with this." He looked up at Kinec, wondering if he would be one of the people who would choose to make the journey to the island—to Indigo's firetale, suddenly so real. "I think if we go to the beach, we'll find boats." His mind was racing, thinking about the possibilities. "Now, will you please go get Michael?"

Kinec looked at him. "He won't like it, you know."

Fisher knew Kinec was right. Michael wanted power a bit more than he wanted what might be good for all the people. "I know."

"Fisher." Kinec swallowed. "If it's true, and there are boats, I'm going."

Fisher grinned. "You and me both, Kinec." He watched, as the boy ran off to find the senior council member of their group. "You and me both," he whispered.

"There are supposed to be six." Rachel counted again. Melissa, Keith, two women and one man she didn't know. "There are only five here."

Jeffrey looked down. "I . . . one of the subjects expired during testing early on." He turned his head and squeezed his eyes shut as though he expected to be slapped.

Rachel didn't understand, at first. She knew what the words meant, but she couldn't believe it was true. "What do you mean, expired?"

"He means they killed someone." Pathik narrowed his eyes at Jeffrey. "Don't you?"

Jeffrey kept his face averted. "It was a very unfortunate accident. It was not anticipated that the test would have that—"

"Just shut up." Rachel was shaking. "Just shut up and get off the boat."

Jeffrey turned and walked away as quickly as his feet would carry him. Rachel watched him go.

"It was Brian." Melissa stared after Jeffrey. "He came the year after I did." She looked at Rachel. "I don't what they did to him, but he never came back one day." Melissa's eyes were dry; there was very little left that could make her cry.

Rachel took Melissa's hand. "I'm sorry."

Melissa nodded. "Me, too." She looked at the men loading supplies onto the boat. "How soon can we leave?"

They kept their word. The whole trip back, Rachel was worried they would try something, blow up the boat in the middle of the passage, or take them someplace else instead of back to the island. But they didn't. The boat landed on the far beach, just like they said it would.

"That map must have scared them but good." Pathik watched as the government men unloaded their supplies onto the beach. "Think we can trust any of that medicine?"

Rachel grinned. "I told Wilkinson the first person that's hurt by anything they send, we mark his location special on a map and send it on to Korusal, with a note identifying him for war crimes. From the look on his face, I think it will be fine." She watched as the pile of supplies grew. "We've got a long way to haul all of that, and not many strong enough to carry much."

Pathik grinned, looking past her at the dunes. "I don't think we'll have such a bad time of it."

Rachel turned and saw twenty, thirty, maybe even forty people streaming toward them. She saw Vivian and Daniel, then Malgam and Nandy. Even Nipper was there, bounding toward them. "How?"

"Da was checking in on us. I thought he might be. I tried to show him what we were up to and he saw!" Pathik grinned, and ran toward his father.

By the time all the supplies had been stowed, Rachel was dead on her feet. "I want to sleep for days." She leaned against Vivian, so exhausted she couldn't hold herself up anymore.

"You deserve to, my love." Vivian smoothed Rachel's hair back from her forehead, staring at her daughter's face as though she couldn't believe she was really seeing it.

"Any word from the beach?" They'd arranged for a watch, day and night, to look out for any boats.

"None." Daniel sat down at the table. He'd just returned from the office. "So far there are no sightings."

"It will take longer from Ganivar." Vivian hoped she was right. "And who knows if anyone from Away will want to come. It could be weeks before they show up, if they do."

"How's Brian's mother?" Rachel had seen the joy as families spotted their lost loved ones, the Honorees they thought were gone forever. She'd watched Sarah stumble toward her father, Keith, and wrap her arms around him, watched another family envelop Melissa, crying and laughing. But one woman had looked and looked, her expression changing from hopeful to worried as she searched the faces. When she heard that the Honoree named Brian had died, she'd fallen to her knees, sobbing inconsolably. Melissa, unlike the rest of the Honorees, could remember most of the people on the island, and she tried to comfort Brian's mother as best she could.

Daniel shook his head. "She was heartbroken. Melissa stayed with her the whole time, and I think Melissa's family made her stay in their unit tonight."

Rachel sighed.

"You worked miracles, Rachel." Vivian stroked her daughter's cheek. "Don't feel bad if you can help it."

Rachel would have told her it was impossible not to feel bad, if she'd still been awake.

Chapter 24

Elizabeth took Jonathan's hand and stepped off the ramp onto the sand. The sun was just rising and it caught the tiny bits of glass, making it look like there was glitter strewn on the beach. "It's beautiful." She looked around at the water, stretching off to the horizon.

"That it is." Jonathan couldn't stop smiling.

The men from the boat dumped their belongings unceremoniously on the beach, and soon the boat was a dot in the ocean.

"I guess that's that." Jonathan chuckled. "They surely wanted quit of us fast."

Elizabeth looked up the beach, then down. It seemed deserted. "I wonder . . ."

"Now don't fret." Jonathan was fretting a bit himself, but he was doing his best to hide it.

"I'm not." Elizabeth turned to Jonathan. "For once, I'm not, Jonathan." She smiled at him. "I want you to know something."

Jonathan looked at her. "Is this a good something?" He shaded his eyes from the glare of the sun. Elizabeth's hair flew out around her head like a halo. It reminded him of days long past, when they were both young. Elizabeth, so beautiful and carefree, her hair loose and waving around her face. Elizabeth when he had first fallen in love with her.

She held out her hands to him and he took them. "It's a good something, I hope." She waited until he was looking in her eyes. "I love you. I know it's late, maybe too late, and I know it's not enough. But I wanted to tell you that, anyway."

Jonathan lowered his chin, so the brim of his hat hid his face. He was silent for a moment. Then, he looked back into her eyes—his Elizabeth. "It's plenty, Elizabeth. It's plenty."

They both heard the shouts at the same time. Turning together, they saw people running down the beach toward them. Elizabeth shaded her eyes, squinting to try to see.

"Is that—"

"It is! It's our Rachel!"

In the evening, after they'd had a chance to rest and unpack some things, Elizabeth and Rachel sat together near the platform, while Jonathan went on a tour of the cave with Daniel.

"I did bring others, but I think this one will do fine, once it can get some sun." Elizabeth inspected the last of the orchid crosses Rachel still had—the other one had died in the dim light of the cave.

"It will get sun tomorrow, then." Rachel grinned. "That's another thing we told them—that we wouldn't hide anymore, here in the cave. The whole island will be ours to wander as we like, to make our home. Pathik and I are thinking we'll build a house out there, up high on the dunes somewhere. And Indigo said there was a wind farm here once. We're going to try to find that—" Rachel broke off, realizing she'd mentioned Indigo's name. "I'm sorry, Ms. Moore."

Elizabeth shook her head. "Don't be sorry, Rachel. He was a special person. We need to remember him as often as we can." She ran her fingers through her hair, enjoying the way it felt. She decided she'd never wear it in a bun again. "Where is Pathik at now?"

Rachel grinned. "Planning Usage. He's going to teach Usage classes, just like Indigo did. He says it's no wonder they got in such a mess here, with no rules about how they use their talents."

"I imagine he's right." Elizabeth frowned. She watched as a gray-haired lady walked past, led by a cherubic-looking young girl. "Certainly Filina could have used some rules." She'd heard about all the things the woman had done.

Rachel followed her gaze. "She can't do any

harm now." Rachel wondered if Filina had any idea what Lethe had done to her. It had happened the day after Rachel, Pathik and the Honorees had returned to the island. Sarah said Lethe had knocked on the door of the unit where Filina lay drugged. Jim had been watching over Lethe since the day of Celebration. He'd gone to the secret unit Filina had kept the girl locked away in and brought her back with him. But he hadn't been with her when she came to see Filina. Later, he said he hadn't told her anything about what Filina had done, or what she'd made Lethe, unwittingly, do.

Sarah said Lethe had just settled next to Filina's bed and asked if she could stay with her for a while. Sarah couldn't see the harm—the woman was the only mother the girl could remember. She'd left to find Jim and when she'd returned with him, Lethe was still sitting next to the bed. She'd turned, looked up at them with a smile on her face. "She won't need to be asleep anymore. I fixed her."

She had, indeed, fixed her. They'd decided to skip Filina's next sedative dose, and when she woke, she had no memory. At least no memory of what she had done, of Celebration, and most importantly, of her own talent. They'd questioned her exhaustively, and she'd shown no sign of knowing anything about those parts of her past.

Sarah was wary, but they had a general meeting about the situation, and everyone agreed to stop the drugs and see what happened. And it was just as Lethe said. Without any recollection of her power, Filina was rendered harmless.

Lethe had been working, slowly, in the days since the Honorees had been returned, to restore their memories. She said it was harder than wiping them, that it took care and attention to detail. But she kept working on it, and she told Jim that she was sure she could give them back everything she had taken. She felt sad that she had done anything at all to them. "They weren't really unhappy at all, were they?"

But when anyone asked her if she would restore Filina's memories, she just shook her head. "Mother was *so* unhappy. She's happier now."

"Ms. Moore." Rachel spoke the words almost shyly. "I wanted to ask you if you would help me start a greenhouse. Here, I mean. Jim and Sarah said they thought they could find some old glass windows—they said there are places on the island where houses are still almost intact. And if we could find the right location . . . well, I was hoping—"

"Why do you want to do that, Rachel?"

"I know it may sound silly, but I think there's a place in life for . . . for just beauty, maybe. For the kind of pleasure beauty can bring, in all its different forms, to the people who see it. And I think we might be ready for that, here. A simple pleasure. One that has nothing to do with survival. It's a sort of magic, if you can reach that place."

"Rachel."

"Yes, Ms. Moore?"

"I think it's time for you to call me Elizabeth."

end

OTHER BOOKS YOU MAY ENJOY

NEW ZAPATA

by

Teri Hall

It's 2052, and there's one less state in the union. Texas, now known as the Republic of Texas, has seceded, just like it did in 1861, though for different reasons this time.

Rebecca lives in New Zapata, a border town in The Republic of Texas. She's nineteen years old, born and raised in the R of T, and doesn't remember a time when things were different, though her Aunt Cathy does. Rebecca's married to Chad, the boy who charmed her into an unplanned pregnancy. She loves her young son, Luke, but she almost died giving birth to him.

That means Rebecca has a problem. Because in New Zapata, birth control and abortion are illegal. So is divorce. And Chad thinks sex is his husbandly right.

There's an underground of sorts in The R of T, and it reaches even as far as sleepy New Zapata. A group of older women--Rebecca's Aunt Cathy and some others--have been gathering under the guise of having Bunco parties to try to help women in Rebecca's position. These ladies remember a time when things were different, when women did have choices.

But it's a dangerous game to defy the R of T. Rebecca and her friends may end up playing for their lives.

HELPER12

by

Jack Blaine

Helper12 works as a Baby Helper in Pre Ward, the place where babies spend their first six months of life before they're tracked for vocations and sent to training. She does her job well, and she stays out of trouble. But one day, the Sloanes, Society members who enjoy all the privileges of their station—family unit clearance, a private dwelling, access to good food and good schools—come to "adopt" one of the

Pre Ward babies. The Director makes a deal and the Sloanes walk out with a brand new child.

They also walk out owning Helper12—the Director sells her to them, and there's nothing she can do but go. At the Sloanes, Helper12 enters a world where people should be able to enjoy life—with high position and riches come the opportunity for individual freedom, even the chance to love—but that's not what she finds. The Sloanes are keeping secrets. So is their biological son, Thomas.

Helper12 has some secrets of her own; she's drawing, which is a violation, since Baby Helpers aren't tracked for Art. And she's growing to love the child she was bought to care for—at the same time that Ms. Sloane is becoming disenchanted with her impulse baby buy.

When all your choices are made for you, how do you make some for yourself? Helper12 is about to find out.

TWITCH

by

Jack Blaine

Twitch was born into the system: the system of Society members and lower designates. Unfortunately for her, she belongs to the latter group. Lower designates are tracked for a task and expected to do what they're told, when they're told, from birth on. Twitch has never known anything different. She lives her life from day to day, working at the Pre Ward, trudging home to the complex at night, following the rules because to defy them means imprisonment, or even death.

Still, when her only real friend mysteriously disappears, Twitch asks one too many questions. She's caught in a trap from which she can't escape, her fate in the hands of a mad man.

But someone notices Twitch—someone cares enough to risk it all to save her. She discovers another world, where secret plans are being laid to overthrow the system and liberate the lower designates. And Twitch has a key role to play. Or does she?

Who do you believe when your life is filled with lies? What is the truth? **Twitch will have to trust someone. Or die trying.**

ABOUT THE AUTHOR

Teri Hall likes to write books.

33816225R00140

Made in the USA
Charleston, SC
19 September 2014